THE EMERALD RIDER

(DRAGONEER SAGA BOOK FOUR)

M.R. MATHIAS

Copyright © 2013 M. R. Mathias
All rights reserved.

ISBN: 1484824008
ISBN 13: 9781484824009

Includes bonus content:
Crimzon and Clover One—Orphaned Dragon, Lucky Girl

This one is for Marlee, Hunter, Cade, KayLynne, Kalyn, and Brady, Dragoneers all. Thanks to Derek Prior for the edit, Anton Kokarev for the cover art, and Kristi and Misty, for the proofing.

PART I
A DANGEROUS VISIT

CHAPTER ONE

Jenka kissed Zahrellion deeply. She was pressing herself against him, as if she could make them melt together in the moment. Jenka didn't mind. He needed this so badly he ached for her. She looked up at him and he took in the way the surreal, cloud-formed room swirled in a perfect cube around them. The soft illumination from his eyes tinted her pale complexion a bright shade of green. Even in this moment of longing, it amazed him that he saw no hint of the tattoos that once marked her face. Her beauty made his heart swell, and in her lavender orbs, he saw the warmest, most comfortable sort of love.

A trace of worry passed across her brow. She lowered her eyes and buried her head in his chest. "You don't even know if it's a boy or a girl." She took a deep breath and hugged him even tighter. "You don't even know."

"Then tell me," he whispered, noticing the darker tint to the clouds churning around them. A flicker of lightning came from a great distance, but the thunder that followed was a long, low grumble which seemed to grow nearer as it lingered.

She squeezed him and let out a long, regretful sigh. "I can't, Jenka." The warmth of her touch was fading. "This is just a dream."

Jenka woke as the first fat drops of rain splattered across his windblown face. He wasn't cold, but it was cool around them. He wasn't sure where he was, but he knew he was on Jade's back. The growing green dragon was winging them across an expanse of untended flatland. The sun was low, and they were flying toward a coppery sunset that revealed the lacy edge of the continent they'd just crossed.

A grumbling roar, from not so far away, caught Jenka's attention, and he looked up to see the yellowed underbelly of a massive red dragon above him. As his heart slowed back down, it all came back to him.

It was Crimzon, and they needed rest. One of the fire drake's wings had been ruined in a battle with a swarm of the savage Sarax beasts. Nothing more than the Dour-fortified spell Rikky Camille had placed on the wing was keeping the old dragon aloft. As far as any of them knew, Rikky's spell could give way at any moment, and he wasn't anywhere near to recast it.

The truth be told, Jenka wasn't sure why it had lasted this long.

The old red had led Jenka and his dragon, Jade, over the mountains of southern Kar, a place Crimzon said he'd reigned over for half a hundred years. By the size of the hoard piled in the cavern in which they'd last slept, Jenka couldn't doubt it. That was several days ago. Now they needed to recoup before crossing another expanse, the last of their long journey.

Out in the sea before them was their destination. In that not-so-distant land, a lifetime ago, Crimzon's rider, Clover, was spelled to stone as bait for a trap. The wizard Xaffer believed that dragons could turn into humans and walk among them. He wanted to make a potion so he could reverse the casting and spell himself into a dragon. He believed he needed the essence of one of these transformed dragons to achieve his end.

Claiming to have knowledge of how to defeat the terrible shark-mawed creatures that were popping up across the land in those days, he lured Crimzon and Clover to his measly temple, petrified Clover, and then put her solid form in a place into which no dragon could fit.

Xaffer had hoped Crimzon would turn himself into a man and come get her. Crimzon, who was even then so wing-wounded he could barely fly, and bound by his rider's wishes, made a bargain with the dwarves and over the course of a decade used their tunnels to traverse the world. Clover had committed Crimzon to battle the Confliction, and more so to prepare the Dragoneers to finish it.

They'd won that war.

Now, Crimzon believed that Jenka, in his Doursaturated state, could pass the wizard's wards and release Clover, especially since Jenka shared a familial bond with Jade. Jenka was determined to give it his all, even though he now knew Crimzon had tricked him. In exchange for summoning the elementals against the alien in the Great Confliction, the old wyrm had made him swear to do this. Jenka, though, knew Crimzon would have called the elementals even had he not sworn. The old dragon had pledged his whole might to that battle long before Jenka or any of the other Dragoneers were born, though, so the subterfuge was forgivable.

Jade was hungry. Jenka could feel the wyrm's gnawing desire to feed. Crimzon was probably ten times hungrier and tired of feeling the pain of exertion. As if reading his thoughts, Crimzon spoke into the ethereal.

"Followsss," he growled before moving into a position ahead of Jade.

Jenka felt his dragon comply and decided that he should rest his eyes some more. He stayed awake for days on end now, and then slept long and hard with the wyrms. It was just one of the many changes that the Dour magic caused in him. Even so, he could not stay awake as long as a dragon could fly, and they'd been flying as long as he could remember.

Soon the rain was a full downpour. They made a circling descent over a long, empty stretch of coastline. Clouds swiftly consumed the sunset and the world grew dark and eerie.

A cavern was visible, but only because Jenka's eyes had grown keener. It opened just above a place where waves crashed into the stony shore, causing huge up-spraying explosions of frothy spume.

No men would bother them there.

It was an angry-looking area, and Jenka decided that if the cavern was empty it would make a perfect place to rest. It would be days before the dragons recouped and were fully sated. He decided correctly that it was where Crimzon was leading them. The old red hated the rain as much as he did and seemed to know exactly where he intended to go. It would definitely be better than this maddening downpour.

The dark hole loomed larger, and as Crimzon swept into it, Jenka felt Jade shiver with both relief and anticipation.

The massive cavity was anything but empty. Most of the jagged surfaces looked razor sharp, but some of them were covered in a softly glowing yellow mold that gave the place just enough illumination to see by, but not much more.

It was all Jenka could do to get dismounted and untether his gear before both wyrms were engaged in a bloody feeding frenzy. The sea cows and rock lions seeking refuge from the storm didn't have a chance. There were hundreds of them. Crimzon was batting with his tail the ones who tried to get away, and Jade was snatching them, crunching them, and then tossing his kills into a pile. He stopped and chugged a smaller morsel down his gullet. Crimzon didn't have to stop. He was chomping a whole sea cow while battering several more of them to death.

In a matter of moments the water sloshing and splashing around the place was pink with blood.

Jenka was tired, but smart enough to let the dragons feed. He scooted away from the sea spray in an attempt to stay dry, but no matter how hard he tried he couldn't shake the lingering dream of Zahrellion and their mysterious child from his mind. It had been plaguing him since they'd left the Frontier, even before the child could have been born. The idea that he was not there, that even had he been there, he could not be a typical father, troubled him deeply.

The baby must have been most of a year old by now. He longed to hold it, to be the father he never had, but he wasn't the same as the mother and child were. He had been saturated with Dour magic so completely that it left its residue all through the very fiber of his being. More than that, he'd assumed some of the alien's existence. He couldn't even venture into a town without causing a confrontation. His very presence put people on edge. No one was comfortable dealing with a man who had glowing coral eyes and could crush them on a whim.

He wasn't sure if he could be a Dragoneer anymore, either. He was so changed that he didn't feel the strength of the connection he'd once had with them. But beyond fulfilling his obligation to Crimzon, his only concern was returning to Zah and their child.

Jenka waited until his bond-mate's bloodlust passed and then got his attention. "Jade!" he yelled, even though he didn't need to. "Before you gorge yourself to slumber, please set me up there." He pointed at a shelf of rock that was a few dozen feet above the damp cavern bottom. "If I am to further fortify Crimzon's wings, I'll need more rest."

"You must need rest, Jenkss," Jade slurred through his gluttonous state. "You can place yourssself theres, if you wisssh."

Jade snaked his head over anyway. Jenka was grateful, because he was too saddle sore and distracted to attempt the simple levitation. Besides that, using the Dour for complex actions made him feel sick and uneasy. He just wanted to rest.

After Jenka dismounted, Jade eyed him for a heartbeat or two. Apparently satisfied that his bond-mate was all right, he went back to his feast. Jenka started a magical blue blaze and stripped out of his wet clothes. No sooner were they laid out did he don some dry ones from his pack and fall soundly asleep to the sounds of crunching bones and ripping flesh.

CHAPTER TWO

Aikira was in a mood.

"Did you bring the weekly?" Zahrellion asked her as she entered the clean but modest sitting room. "They're supposed to have the conclusion to the Piebald Egg story."

They were staying in a small, but opulently furnished, stronghold at Three Forks. It was the best location for a kingdom seat. There were a dozen construction projects going on, including a proper castle, but it was still several years from completion. Without the vermin to harry progress, the "Expansion," or whatever it had now turned into, was unhindered. Towns were springing up down all three of the tributaries, and goods were needed.

The Frontier was thriving.

"They do have it." Aikira forced a smile. "You'll like the way it ends."

When she was around Zahrellion these days, Aikira felt like a servant to a queen, not a sister Dragoneer. It wasn't Zah. It was everyone else out here beyond the kingdom's wall. They treated Zah like royalty because she was royalty. They treated Aikira like an ebony-skinned Outlander, which was like being a three-headed dog to the mainland commoners who'd never traveled the islands.

King Richard had proclaimed Jenka King of the Frontier, and since Zahrellion was Jenka's lover and the mother of his child, history said she was now some sort of Queen Regent.

The only person who disliked it more than Aikira was Zah, though, which sort of evened out the roles they were forced to play until Jenka returned… if he ever returned.

The people treated Aikira like a noble, but every time she mounted Golden, everyone, even Marcherion and Rikky, thought she was doing Zahrellion's bidding, which she mostly was, and that just made it worse. To break the monotony, she was determined to go hunting with the boys this afternoon. She and Golden would remind them what an Outlander girl could do.

She waited while Zahrellion read, but only until the nurse brought in the baby. Golden-haired

Lemmy was with them as always. Since he was a mute, he'd written a sworn statement to be Jericho's protector until Jenka returned.

Jericho was just a year old. He was as beautiful as a baby could be, with a good temperament and an easy grin. He had his father's unmistakable deep green eyes, and could squeeze your finger until it hurt. Crawling now, he was a handful, so Aikira kissed his pink head and spoke into Lemmy's ear.

"She will be well irritated if she reads too long. I've told the nurse to tell her there is a widower and his young daughter from the peninsula hoping to have audience about something or another. They looked desperate but have patiently been waiting their turn. I think they are some of Richard's forgotten nobility looking for help or some-such."

As soon as Lemmy grunted that he understood, Aikira eased off while Zah was immersed. She really didn't want to be around if Zahrellion read past her serial.

The story scribed beneath the one Zah was reading was about the lack of authority on the kingdom's side of the wall. King Richard didn't concern himself with the affairs on the continent anymore. Not as long as the resources he needed kept going to King's Island. The story would have the readers believe guilds, gangs, and witches all vied like lunatics over games of chance, potions, and lust over there. Worse, the story spoke of the vile things King Richard was rumored to be doing to people deep in his dungeon. Things like Gravelbone had done to him. It made Aikira shiver just thinking about it.

Aikira had to admit Midwal was becoming more and more like a sailor's town every day, but not nearly as bad as the story depicted. Zahrellion definitely needed to talk to King Richard, but she wouldn't travel to the islands willingly. Aikira would stand beside her when the time came for that confrontation, but she wasn't in the mood for politics, or tales of the kingdom's abandonment, this day. Today she was determined to hunt vermin with Rikky and March.

* * *

The sound that woke Jenka was terrible. The roar reverberated around the great cavern, drowning out the waves and the grunting barks of the sea life still braving the rocks. It was Crimzon, and he was in tremendous pain.

As quickly as he could shake the cobwebs of slumber from his head, Jenka met Jade and rode his dragon's neck over to where Crimzon lay.

"It'sss coming undone, Jenka," the old wyrm hissed.

Jenka knew he meant Rikky's spell was unraveling. He didn't panic. Instead, he climbed onto hot brimstone scales and positioned himself on Crimzon's back near the wing joints. He almost fell when the great red shifted suddenly and let out another anguished roar. Jade helped him hold steady with his tail, and without further hesitation Jenka reached into his well of alien-infused Dour and let it start flowing through him.

Hurrysss, he heard Jade whisper, but he was already sinking into the magic.

Crimzon's wings had been gnawed by a swarm of Sarax more than once. Worse, the wyrm had stayed in a cavern down a dwarven flue for some fifty-odd years, waiting for the Dragoneers to find their time. The lengthy inaction hadn't helped. Rikky had somehow spelled the wings and muscles in a way that allowed Crimzon to fly, if awkwardly. Rikky understood healing, though, and the loss of limbs. Jenka understood neither. He had only been fortifying Rikky's spell, which was a simple task, if taxing. Now that wouldn't be enough.

Jenka grasped the complexity of Rikky's casting just as the last tendrils of it faded away. He used the Dour to try to reproduce the spell, but wasn't skilled enough. He cursed himself for having a hundred times the power but not the knowledge to accomplish what the old red needed.

Jenka knew Crimzon had his own reasons for helping the Dragoneers in the past; it wasn't just because Clover would have wished it. He had helped them selflessly. If the truth were told, Crimzon's knowledge and his elemental allies had really won the day against that morphing alien thing. Jenka wouldn't allow himself to give up so easily.

With his teeth gnashed tightly and his brow furrowed, he struggled and toiled long into the night and the next day. He put forth every ounce of effort he could summon, and then let his will carry him further, but it wasn't meant to be. He found a way to end Crimzon's suffering, but couldn't make the old red's wings work again. He just didn't have the ability.

Making sure the wyrm wouldn't be in pain became the priority. As he labored on, his dragon's consciousness, and then Crimzon's, crept into his mind.

Enough, Jade said softly.

I can survives heresss, Crimzon said into the ethereal. *These fat sea cows will swim right into my maw. You mussst find her and free her without me.*

I... I... I'm sorry, Crimzon, Jenka's mind stammered. *We are so close.*

You haven't failed me, Jenkass, Crimzon sighed. An eternity of frustration was revealed in the sound. *You ssswore to free Clovers, not nursse me along. Xaffer'sss tower is on the northern end of the land we spoke of. It is a full day's flight from here.*

What... what should I do when I get there? Jenka was extremely spell weary. He was fading.

Xaffer wasss powerful, but he won't have sssurvived this long. The Soulstone, however, may still be bound to the traps he created with it. It isss a powerful device the wizard used to pit men against the demonsss they sssummoned into hisss arena.

How will I know her? asked Jenka.

Clover will seem like a ssstatue, but even still, sshe will ssseem fierce and beautiful. Most likely he kept her in the lower level of the ssstructure. But be wary. Xaffer was clever and he had a following. He created all of this so his priests could battle demons. He will have set unpredictable pitfallsss on the whole place, and Clover's form, too. The Dour flowing through you will absssorb a lot of his mayhem. He will have had to bind a demigod or a demon to his final wardsss. He may have even—

Crimzon's voice continued, but a great exhaustion consumed Jenka, and the slackening flow of Dour he was riding carried him gently into slumber.

When Jade woke Jenka some days later, Crimzon was sleeping so soundly that Jenka didn't bother with the old wyrm. A generation or two had come and gone since the dragon left his rider here. Crimzon would be of little more help. When Jade lowered his head for mounting, Jenka reluctantly left his concerns behind and set out to find Clover and release her.

It was what he had sworn to do.

CHAPTER THREE

What the heck did you hear? Rikky asked Marcherion with his mind. *I don't understand what you mean.*

They were flying over the Frontier at a leisurely pace, each eyeing the mostly wooded terrain for movement as they went. March was riding his fire wyrm Blaze, and Rikky was on the smaller, quicker Silva. It was late spring and both boys were restless. The only excitement they'd had since they destroyed the alien was hunting vermin, and even that was starting to lose its appeal.

Crimzon roared out last night, is what I'm telling you. March looked like he hadn't slept at all. His long brown hair was a tangle, and the clothes under his plated leather riding vest were rumpled and creased. He hadn't even bothered to fully lace the armor.

Are you sure you didn't just fart in the middle of a dream? Rikky laughed. *Were you drinking that harsh stuff again?*

I only drank that stuff once, and it wasn't a fart. March was clearly mad that Rikky wouldn't take him seriously, but he couldn't keep from laughing. Rikky was glad, because when March got mad these days things went downhill quickly.

Only a few days ago March had sheared one of Swineherd's pens in two trying to kill a lone goblin who'd managed to ping his head with a rock and then elude him.

Listen, you one-legged giboon, March barked.

Rikky had to hold his mirth in check.

March was rubbing at the fresh knot as he went on. *Crimzon, who disappeared when Jenka did, roared out last night. Blaze heard it plainly. We asked Crystal and Golden both if they heard it, and just after it happened, too. I can't understand why just Blaze and I would—*

Probably because they are both fire drakes, Rikky observed.

I didn't think of that.

Figures.

After a few moments of March not getting the jibe, Rikky sighed. *Can you tell where it came from? I don't think we can just ignore it, not if you're sure.*

I'm certain. Blaze is certain. It was Crimzon and he was anguished. Locating the source of the call, though... I can sense it. I doubt I could point a place on a map, but Blaze—

I cans finds Crimzonss, Blaze interrupted. *I think we mussst.*

Wait a minute. We? Rikky asked. *Zah is a queen now, and a mother. She can't leave. And Aikira is the Outland Ambassadora. The Dragoneers can't just leave the people of the Frontier. King Richard won't help them at all.*

Weee, the red dragon hissed. *Usss.*

Just then a pair of newly uncocooned horn-heads went darting through the trees below. Silva, who had been hunting, not listening, dove after them. It was all Rikky could do to hold on as she snaked herself out of the sky. They went streaking straight at the forest, with only the slightest bit of angle in their descent. Then, with a sudden down-pressing inertia that threatened to send Rikky into blackness, Silva leveled out and took them skimming over the treetops.

Rikky nearly tumbled off of her backward as he twisted and tried to free his bow from its straps. *You'll have to make another run, Sil,* he said as they passed over the fleeing vermin.

Yesss, the sleek, pewter-scaled wyrm responded, and then banked around.

Marcherion didn't need a second pass. He put an arrow right through one of the creature's vitals. It would die swiftly from the poison with which the shafts were tipped. As would the other one, now that Rikky had his weapon ready.

Rikky loosed as they came out of their arcing turn and almost missed the beast entirely. He didn't like using a regular bow, but the one with Silva's tear mounted in it did far too much damage to use on a typical hunt. This arrow tore through one of the creature's arms. It didn't even slow its gait as it continued to flee. Rikky counted up to nine before it pitched forward into a tumbling heap.

There! I saw something over there. March pointed.

Blaze was already winging his bulk that way. Silva had to bank around again but came out of the turn in an undulating fury of wing beats that carried them right past the larger fire wyrm. They topped a high section of trees and saw a vast orchard spread across a shallow valley. The tree rows cut across in a perfect diagonal, and the scent of nectars, or maybe peaches, filled his nose. Before he could think, a boulder the size of a barrel keg was coming right at them. Silva swerved, and Rikky hugged himself tight against her. He felt it grind over him, but managed to stay seated.

They didn't escape harm. Rikky was spared being maimed, but the rock skimmed across Sliva's rump and tail and sent her careening into the dirt along a row of fully grown fruit trees. Before they hit, Rikky saw an ogre as tall as the trees around it. It was about to swing a branch at Blaze, who was just now topping the ridge.

Hold on, Rikkysss, Silva hissed into the ethereal. Rikky hoped the warning reached the others, for he was in no position to call them. Limbs and leaves and whipping branches tore at his face. A very firm peach splattered across his neck and he was coated with the spray of another that impacted Silva's scales and exploded. Rikky doubted he could hold on any harder than he was.

Not so badss. It—cras— The voice in Rikky's head stopped suddenly.

Rikky's heart dropped to his bowels. Losing the connection with his bond-mate so abruptly scared him. For that instant he wasn't sure if she was dead or just knocked unconscious. Then she was there again, angry and grunting as they ground to a stop.

Instinctually, they both were feeling for injury in the dragon's wings. Luckily, Silva wasn't hurt from the crash, but the boulder had bruised quite deeply the area where her tail met her body. She used those muscles to keep her balance in the air.

"Fuuu—" March yelled as he and his dragon went flying by.

The ogre had missed them and was now storming down the lane formed by the tree rows. It had the branch held overhead now and was roaring. Its eyes were locked on Rikky, or maybe Silva, who was gathering herself behind her dislodged rider.

Rikky's first thought was that an ogre shouldn't be trying to harm them; then he saw the charred ring at its neck and knew that it was one of the many ogres the Druids of Dou had collared and mindwashed. It wasn't a comforting thought. Worse, the thing had been feasting on peaches and was in some sort of rage. It would try to defend the bountiful trees, as if they belonged to it.

Rikky realized he had an arrow drawn. The poison it was tipped with only affected the alien-blooded creatures. To this ogre it was just a shaft, but Rikky let it fly nonetheless, and then half-charged, half-hopped on his steel-shod, wooden peg leg into the next tree row as Silva met the beast.

When Rikky turned to see what was happening, he found his dragon hadn't faced down the ogre at all, but instead had shimmied into another tree row and tripped the thing with her tail.

The ogre went sprawling and took down a few trees as it went. Then Marcherion and Blaze were landing and Rikky knew to stay exactly where he was. *Lie flat, Silva!* he called with his mind. *Lie as flat as you can.*

Yesss, she hissed, then a roaring gout of dragon flames, and the sizzling hum of March's eye-rays drowned out everything, save for the sound of falling trees and the keening screams of the dying ogre.

CHAPTER FOUR

Jenka figured the knowledge he'd gathered from the alien shape-shifter was his own burden to bear. How could he explain to the other Dragoneers that there were other worlds, on other planets? Jenka had seen them through the memories and mind of the shape-shifter.

He knew.

Zahrellion, who was a schooled druida, and Aikira, who knew wizardry, might grasp it, but March and Rikky would only act like they did.

Even though the creature that crashed his vessel here wasn't fond of much anything other than feeding, Jenka decided that some of those worlds out there would be pleasant. The creature's limited thought process gave Jenka's glimpse of it all a narrow perspective.

The fact that he understood his insight was limited was a testament to the wealth of understanding he and Jade had gathered, though. Neither had to use mental or physical voice to communicate; not even the ethereal was needed these days. They were an extension of each other, at least when they were both awake and flying. The connection between them when they weren't in physical contact was still heightened, but not so much. No, Jenka reflected. His memory was a wavering flicker of images all lensed in green. He knew his bond with Jade had been that way before the alien, since even before they and Rikky had slain Gravelbone.

As it often did now, Jenka's mind drifted to some random place from his past. This time it was the sky above Mainsted, where Jenka's half-brother, Prince Richard, sacrificed his soul and the eternity of his beloved dragon, Royal, for the sake of the kingdom. Then even those thoughts faded, and Jenka sat in a daze as the wind flowed through his untended mess of brown hair.

It was a beautiful day. He didn't know if it was spring or fall on this part of the planet, but it was clearly one of those two seasons. Considering the rotation and alignment of the orb over which he was suspended sent his mind off again. The vastness of space, and the idea that they were but a speck in it, consumed him. That lasted for some time.

The constellations and swirling bands of circular light he and his wyrm were gliding through slowly faded into clouds, which faded into something else.

Now it was Zahrellion occupying his mind. Slender and beautiful, her white hair, lavender eyes, and delicate skin still radiated exotic beauty, but then his mind applied the tattoos to her face. Circles and squares on her cheeks and a triangle on her forehead the color of old, dark wood. *No, wait,* Linux had the darker triangle; he was... he was... He is in a different body than his own now. And King Blanchard?

As Jade carried them over the sea, Jenka's mind drifted even farther away. He might have fallen into a full state of reverie had Jade not trumpeted a snort of disdain at a flock of giant sea dactyls that ventured too close.

When he cleared his head, Jenka found that they were closing in on a land mass that was more like a small continent than an island. An endless strand of white, sugary sand lined an emerald green shore. A few cattle-pens, built from stacked stones, could be made out inland. The land along the shore, though, seemed like some wintery tundra full of random drifts speckled with thin clumps of prickly-looking scrub. It wasn't snow. The sand was just that white. The contrast with the almost glowing seashore was a wonder within itself.

They rose in the sky and followed the seemingly deserted beach from a considerable height. They didn't want to come upon a town or village and cause a stir. Then they saw a few fishing boats outside a small inlet, and what might have been a village. The road leading away from the huddle of structures went straight inland as far as the eye could see. As they continued, the shore grew rockier, but no less spectacular in color, for a few dozen yards out from the rising land was a reef just under the surface of the sea.

The colors of his eyes, Jade hissed in awe.

Jenka heard the musing, even though Jade hadn't meant it for him. He considered that his eyes were so unnatural that his dragon would have that thought. It made him feel alien. Like he was the only one of his kind and always would be.

As they continued north, Jenka wondered what would be waiting for them. He didn't have to wonder long, for there was a great temple built on a prominence that thrust itself proudly out of the sea like the bow of a gargantuan ship. Sitting just beside it, like some forgotten ruin, was a smaller rock building with a more modest tower. Jenka figured that was Xaffer's old abode, but getting there now presented other problems.

You'll have to let me off and I'll creep into the sanctuary, Jenka suggested. The sun was getting low in the sky. It would be dark soon. *There, over by those woods, but wait until full dark.*

Yesss, Jade grumbled out what might have been a laugh. *But you can ussse the Dour to get there, Jenksss.*

I'm not comfortable teleporting and levitating, he replied.

Someday sssoon you may have to use the Dour. I would rather you tempered yourssself to the task than let it overwhelm you in a moment of crisssis, Jade lectured. *I will land on the cliffs below the temple and wait for your call. Return before the sunrise or I will come for you.*

Let's search from the sky before dark falls, and no, give me three days before you come storming.

The third sunrise, then?

Yes.

A bit of circling and studying the terrain revealed that a sizable city separated the temple grounds from the rest of the land, and a sizable vineyard separated the city from the temple.

The idea that there was an arena under the temples, and that demons and magicked men once fought there, was hard to believe, but the layout looked as if it were designed for defense, or maybe containment.

They concentrated their spying on the grounds of the newer temple, for the symbol in its courtyard was a larger version of the one in the older building's open bailey. There were a half-dozen black-robed men doing precise movements in two rows of three. Another figure in a gray robe trimmed in olive green mirrored them, or led them, through the routine. They all had a staff and, what with the twirling and jabbing they were doing, they looked as if they could use them handily. Jenka hoped they wouldn't notice his intrusion into the old place. He would follow Jade's advice and use the Dour to get by them. They wouldn't be able to see him, much less confront him, if he was invisible.

It may be a few levels deep, Jade, Jenka voiced. *It may take me a while to find her and then a longer while to try to free her.*

We must try all we can try, Jade offered. *But if we cannot free her, we must end her. We promissssed to let her suffer no more.*

Yesss, Jenka responded, and noticed curiously that he'd slurred his response just like his dragon sometimes did.

Jade only chuckled and then turned them around for another pass over the temple.

CHAPTER FIVE

Rikky looked up to see another ogre charging down the tree lane at him. It was a long way away yet, but no less menacing. It was a female, with filthy olive-skinned breasts the size of flour sacks bouncing crazily as it came. Hobbling through the soft dirt over toward his dragon, he crossed out of that tree row into the next. That was when he realized there was yet another ogre in the area. It was not much bigger than a man, but twice as thick of limb, and it was right there walloping him into the dirt.

Things went black, but only for a moment. He was able to roll away from the next blow. He then managed to crawl out of the creature's reach.

Two things happened next: Silva thumped the juvenile creature into a tree trunk with her tail, and the thing's mother crossed into the row just in time to see it happen.

The mother ogre literally ran up Silva's bulk, bear-hugged her neck just under her head, and began choking her. Rikky had no idea where his bow was. He never carried a sword when they went hunting because Marcherion always handled the blade work at the end. March said he liked it, but Rikky knew that March just wanted to save him from having to dismount over and over again in the field. Nevertheless, there he stood with no weapon at all as an ogre was violently choking his bond-mate.

Rikky struggled to stand up. *March!* He screamed into the ethereal. He hobbled over to the nearest tree and leaned against it for support. From there he tried to see where his bow was. He saw Silva swing her neck around and bash the clinging ogre into a tree. It was a savage impact but the creature didn't let go. Worse, Silva looked to be fading from the fight.

Where are you, March? Rikky screamed, his heart hammering into a panic. He could feel Silva's need to draw breath. He knew she was nearly done. "MAAARRRCCCHHH!"

I'm here, a musical voice responded. It wasn't Marcherion, but it was just as welcome.

Rikky looked up to see Golden sweep past Silva's upper body. The glittering dragon ripped the ogre across its back. Three slices started like dripping lines, but slowly opened into deep scarlet furrows.

Silva shook the ogre off then, or it fell off, for she wasn't doing much shaking. Rikky limped over to her with tears flooding his eyes. He'd been helpless. Like a lump. He loved his dragon, though, and he was relieved beyond measure that she was starting to recover.

March needs me, Aikira voiced. *A limb punctured Blaze's wing skin. He's stuck in an awkward position. The younger ogre is hiding now, two rows over. Watch yourself.*

I will. Rikky ran his hand over Silva's pewter-plated brow. He could see his bow lying a few dozen strides away now but wasn't ready to leave his dragon. He took a deep breath and then began exploring her wounds. He healed what he could, but Silva's delicate esophagus was almost crushed and would take a long time before it was anywhere close to normal. Rikky was certain he would have to have the butchers at the keep grind her deer meat so she could swallow it.

He saw the other ogre once, as it darted out of the area. It was probably scared witless being without a mother for the first time.

March, are you all right? Rikky asked. *Is Blaze?*

It's just a tear, but we were stuck, Marcherion finally responded. *We ended two more of the druids' lot.*

I think the membrane will line up well enough, Aikira added. *We're coming to you. How is Silva?*

She won't be feasting for a while, but she will live.

Musst spell the membranes for usss, Blaze hissed.

Before Rikky could respond, Crystal, Zahrellion's frost dragon, sent a shrill shriek of warning echoing across the ethereal.

By the time Rikky was mounted and Silva had struggled herself into the air, the others were gone. He and his dragon could not have felt more helpless.

* * *

Zahrellion was in the stronghold's great hall hearing the concerns of a man who had once been contracted to make tack for King Blanchard's stablemaster in Mainsted. He seemed like a good man, a man who was once proud of his work, and proud of his place in the scheme of things. The filthy little girl beside him was clutching a doll and crying simply because her father was so upset. One look at her huge, sad eyes melted Zahrellion's heart. The streaks from the tears running down her face were the cleanest parts of her.

The man was not proud now. In fact, he was on his knees begging for employment, sobbing about the home he'd lost, and how his beautiful young wife had just disappeared. Zahrellion was going to help them. She was just waiting for him to calm down. She'd already gotten the scribe's attention to take her command but couldn't bring herself to interrupt the man's desperation. Jericho was sleeping in a basket beside Lemmy at a nearby table, and the pair of door guards were patiently keeping another petitioner from entering.

No one expected what happened next.

The little girl started wiggling. Then she started doing a silly twirling dance. The man's pitiful voice droned on and on, and then suddenly his form expanded and shifted. The little girl disappeared in a roiling cloud of smoke. Then a terrible black maw attached to some ever-changing predatory form launched itself at Zah.

Zahrellion's protective instinct forced her to check what was happening to her son. What she saw made her icy blood burn. There was the girl, who was now a young witchy-looking woman, all bedecked in a high-collared gown and garish face paint, reaching for Jericho. Before she could think, she screamed out to her dragon, who shrieked out across the ethereal as she'd been told to do.

Lemmy's long, thin blade would have cleaved the woman's head, had she been in a fleshy form. As it was, the elven steel passed right through her.

The woman cackled at this, but only until she realized Lemmy wasn't deterred. Lemmy had Jericho by the wrist and was yanking him toward the hall's service door.

Zah met the closing jaws before her with an ear-pummeling blast of yellow Dou magic. Even though she was no longer associated with the defunct order of druids, the magic she'd learned there was hers to command. The bespelled man was flung into the rock wall and was partially buried in the crumble Zah's blast caused.

The witch, however, was between Lemmy and the service door now. It was clear Lemmy's sword didn't scare her at all. She waved her arms crazily and then shouted a word that seemed to leave her mouth like a fist. Lemmy was knocked backward so hard it looked as if his skeleton was crushed flat against the wall.

Jericho was left sitting on the floor before the witch, unprotected.

It all happened so fast that the two door guards were just starting into the room. The next petitioner wasn't who he seemed either, though. The guards were yanked backward from the middle by unseen hands and left on the floor screaming and bleeding from the holes left in their abdomens.

Zahrellion wanted more than anything to blast the young raven-haired bitch who dared attack her and her son, but the witch was holding Jericho now. There was little she could do that wouldn't harm him, too. She was suddenly so afraid for her son that she wanted to scream.

PART II
XERRIN FYL

CHAPTER SIX

*J*enka cocked his head curiously and took a long, deep breath. It was dark. The sun had long since faded into the sea. He was standing at the steel-banded door of Xaffer's old temple. There were no guards posted. He couldn't even spot a sentry. Jade had let him off at the edge of the vineyards, a short walk away. It wouldn't have mattered if there was a full brigade watching the place, though. Jenka was invisible and would be for half of the night or more.

What piqued him as he stood there was the sudden feeling that this might be the end of him.

Nooss, Jenkas, Jade hissed. *You will triumph here.*

Three days, he said as he reached to test the door. It wasn't locked and the hinges were surprisingly quiet for their age. After he stepped in, he pushed the door closed behind him and concentrated.

Jade?

Yesss.

Good, I still feel you there. He'd been worried about the place being warded from the ethereal. He also worried about getting lost in some wizard's maze and just drifting away in his Doursaturated head. Having Jade in his mind with him would go far toward keeping him centered and on task. Determined to help Clover now, he worked at keeping his thoughts focused.

Inside, the temple was amazingly well kept. In fact it seemed as if the lobby had been recently full of men. He wasn't sure how he sensed that, but he did. Maybe it was just the fact that the small oil lamps ensconced in the walls were lit? Still, whoever had been here hadn't used the front door. It wasn't like the rest of the place. He hadn't noticed any paths or wear marks in the lawn between the two buildings, either.

He figured there was an underground or hidden hall built between the buildings. It was the most logical explanation.

The rest of the ground floor was about what he'd expected it to be, only the wooden pews weren't dusty, they were freshly oiled, and the scent of hot candle wax was heavy in the air. One look at the altar revealed why. Hundreds, maybe thousands of red and black candles had been melted there over the years. The sides of the navel-high block were caked with it, and it had built up and puddled along the floor in a strange, misshapen glob.

There was another room beyond the main hall, and the stairs opened into it. They led away, going both up and down in a tight spiral. Jenka went down, and down, and down. Four floors down. The first two landings had been well kept and were illuminated with lamps, but the third floor was cavernous and dark, as if it had a vaulted ceiling that opened up through the floor, or maybe floors, above. Then there was the final level, where the cobwebs were as thick as the rat droppings.

There were no torches or lamps here. He could see well enough, though. The Dour flowing through him heightened all of his senses, but none more than his eyes. Everything was bathed in an eerie emerald light. It was like each separate block of stone was radiating its own field.

He was compelled to draw the sword Mysterian had made for him. It had the crystallized tear of Jade's mam mounted in its hilt. Jenka also had Clover's teardrop in a pouch at his hip. He had enough contained Dour to level a city and the means to use it. None of that mattered, though, for the moment he stepped onto the lowest floor he knew he'd activated some sort of spell.

Then he realized it was more of a release than anything. That, and he wasn't invisible anymore. A heavy slab slid down over the landing behind him, blocking him from the way he'd come. Then a long, slow growl echoed from the depths of the darkness. Looking around him, he decided this was probably the right place to be. Whatever it was that just came to life was most likely warded to guard something down here, and it didn't sound pleased about his intrusion.

There was nothing to do but follow the sound. A hallway led in the right direction, and he cautiously started down it. No more than three paces in, he had to clear away a spider as big as his fist from a web that was blocking the way.

Beyond the web there was a single door on the right. It was painted the sort of red you see on the fingertips of night girls. The stuff was as glossy as if it had just been brushed on, but everything around it was grimy and coated with dust. A dozen paces farther down the hall, he passed another door which was exactly the same. He went on, and again there was another glossy red door. When he looked back, and ahead, he saw that the corridor was infinite and that there were evenly spaced red doors all the way down it. The spider web he'd cut away wasn't behind him, either. Understanding he was in some sort of trap, he stepped over to the door before him and cautiously put his ear to it. He was rewarded with a savage howl that might have come from just the other side.

Since Jenka had been swallowed by the alien, he'd been torn between his love for Zahrellion and his sense of duty. There was no emotional tie to what he was doing, and there was a sea of regret for leaving his love and his unborn child behind, but he was here. Any reservations he might have had over opening the red door were numbed by his lack of enthusiasm. He never expected to survive the alien. How could he hesitate here, when the Dour itself and his word to Crimzon had combined in a moment of triumph to keep him alive for just this purpose? He didn't know the answer, so he opened the door and made ready to jab with his sword anything that might be lurking.

Beyond the door was an impossible chamber that was as big as the old temple itself. It was a long-sided octagonal, and the walls were easily twice as tall as Jenka. It seemed that he was standing inside a dome, save for the space wasn't under a round roof. The four square panels that formed over him were solid. The four triangular panels, at each corner of the peak, were made of stained glass, and beyond them the sun, or some simulated source of light, glowed brightly. In the square surface that was parallel to the floor, the same symbol he'd seen in the courtyards was displayed. He looked down to find it was on the floor as well. Turning slowly, he saw that he was in the center of an arena. The door behind him was gone, and there across the slightly bowled floor was a bearish creature the size of a house. Its burning cherry eyes were narrowed, and its toothy snout was frothing with anticipation. Bristles quivered and rippled over its bulging muscles. It had claws as long as knives, and a long, spiked tail, which was whipping around. It started sauntering toward him. Jenka had no idea how to defeat such a thing. He doubted it could be done with a sword.

He could outmaneuver the creature and maybe tire it, but with so much Dour at his disposal that would be foolish.

He couldn't decide if this were some illusionary monster or if it had been summoned and bound to Xaffer's spell. He also wondered if Clover's statue was even down here anymore. This was a place where huge things did battle, not a place to keep a petrified woman. There were long, gouged scratches in the walls, and the few large stone blocks that were spaced about the outer combat area were busted and scattered.

This was something real.

There was nowhere to hide, save for huddling behind some rubble, so he ran toward the center of the bowl, trying to steel himself to the fact that he was about to have to use the Dour. When he did, the priests, or monks, or whatever those robed men were who worshipped here, would probably feel it. As the surge of sparkling energy flowed through his guts and slowly down each limb, he decided the worshipers above would be wise to stay out of it. If they tried to stop him, he didn't know what he would do to them.

CHAPTER SEVEN

Zahrellion was dumbfounded by the witch's attack, but Crystal was quick and not so surprised. A walled-in area had been designated for the dragons when they were in Three Forks, and Crystal could cover the distance between it and the stronghold with one chilly flap of her wings. As Zahrellion fought to hold back her pulse of devastating magic, Crystal's head burst through the window behind the attack, taking part of the sill and frame with it.

Lemmy was striding across the polished tile floor, a silent scream of frustration on his fair face, his sword bared and ready. The pitiful man-thing that had been with the witch was writhing on the floor and slowly pulling back into its natural form. Lemmy's blade must have found it, for a puddle of thickening black fluid was spreading around it.

The witch was forced to turn away from Lemmy's charge to see what was behind her. In that instant, Lemmy dove with all the half-elven grace he had in him. He hit the floor, rolled twice, and then slid up to his feet, somehow snatching the baby at the very moment the shock of dragon fear consumed the witch. He didn't stop, either. He took Jericho straight across the room and out into the quickly emptying entry hall.

Crystal's huge maw came clacking down over the beautiful woman, and Zah found she had to close her eyes because she didn't want to see almost perfect beauty destroyed in such a violent manner. It was an unnecessary thing and keeping them open might have saved her the blow she took next, but now she was sailing backward across the hall. The witch had turned herself to mist, slipped out of the way of Crystal's teeth and blasted Zah so hard in the gut with a fist of energy that she couldn't even breathe.

Zahrellion landed hard, and her head whipped back, smacking the marble blocks that served as interior walls. She ended up in a heap, half-conscious and trembling. Only the rage building inside her dragon, which she could feel plainly inside herself as well, kept her from slipping away.

Smoke can be frozen, witchesss, Crystal hissed before glacializing the now misty form of the voluptuous woman.

For a long, slow moment it looked as if the dragon was correct. The witch's form began to slow and stiffen as it hovered over the floor, but then the raven-haired woman's jaw clenched tight, her eyes closed, and she began to tremble and convulse. Zahrellion couldn't do anything if she tried. She was clinging to consciousness by Crystal's will alone.

All of a sudden, the witch burst into flames; flames encased in ice that melted away in a matter of heartbeats.

"You foolish breed whore," the witch spat. "I am Ankha Vira from the Coven Wisteria, and you and King Richard will keep the people united or we will eliminate the both of you and reform the Council of Three with the true heir to the throne. The Coven of Hazeltine has withered to naught. Wisteria will have a seat. We have taken control of the peninsula, and we intend to keep it. Watch yourself well or the Frontier and little Jericho will become ours to shape and mold as well."

Zah wanted to shout back at her, but Ankha Vira was gone. Zah was recovering, at least enough to get to her feet. Her anger mingled with Crystal's and she gained resolve, if not strength, with every step she took. By the time Marcherion and Aikira came storming in, she was in a full state of indignant rage.

"Where were you?" she yelled at Aikira. "You're supposed to be here. You have duties."

Then to March, "And you, the one who is always acting like some commander of defenses. Where were you when Prince Jericho was attacked?"

"Where was his father?" Marcherion's words came out sharp, like a sword jab, and pierced Zahrellion's heart. She was no less angry with Aikira, though. Aikira was supposed to carry a message to King Richard on King's Isle for her. It would certainly be a different message now.

March glared at her, then stalked a few steps away. He called over his shoulder, "Tell Rikky that Blaze and I are more suited for the task. He'll know what I'm talking about."

It was clear he was speaking to Aikira because Zahrellion had no idea to what he was referring.

Aikira waited until March was gone. She stayed the half-dozen guards at the door with the palm of her hand and then began searching for words.

Zahrellion was expecting an apology, but that isn't what she got.

"Listen to me, Zahrellion. I am not your subject, nor your servant." Aikira's vehement tone took Zahrellion off guard. "My dragon and I are not here to run messages for some half-arsed queen of the sticks. I'm sorry this happened, but if you and Jericho were up in Clover's castle, instead of playing ruler of the land, like March and Herald have been suggesting, this wouldn't have happened. I am sick of it. I am going to help Marcherion with our real duty. Rikky will explain."

Zahrellion didn't understand. She was just trying to do what everyone wanted her to do. After a long, deep breath, she found the only thing that mattered to her at that moment was Jericho.

Without another thought she ran off to find Lemmy and her son.

* * *

Jade sat on a perch, watching below as a pelican dove after a dark school of smaller fish. Like some elongating and ever-shifting shadow, the knot of minnows turned and darted and circled round under the surface. Against the pale, green-tinted sand, they were impossible to miss.

Jade didn't envy the fish. Not only was the pesky pelican diving in to fill his bill, but underneath the school there were a handful of larger feasters. These shot through the denser part of the mass and filled their maws at will.

A few wingbeats away there was a darker area. The minnows were trying to get there so they could dive into the depths. Jade watched all of this with a growing sense of accomplishment building inside him. He was strong now, easily as strong as Silva and Golden. He'd flown halfway around the world and had been forced to maneuver through every kind of current imaginable. His sense of navigation had grown powerful, and he was confident he could find every single place he had ever been again, if the need arose.

He knew his mamra would be proud of him, and he almost shed a tear at her memory. Only a sudden, shocking development with the fish below saved him from it.

As the ever-shrinking knot of fish finally found the deeper area, something large, an eel-like shape, darted out and snatched three of the bigger fish that had been feeding on the minnows. The pelican had to stall mid-dive, which Jade knew wasn't easy at all, but the bird managed to avoid the scene. Jade wondered if the school of minnows hadn't been luring the bigger fish in for the eel all along.

CHAPTER EIGHT

The humongous beast seemed less like a bear now that it was there and clawing at him. Jenka decided it was more like a badger, for it was lightning quick and unafraid of the softly glowing Dour he radiated. He got a good slice in, and a good look in the thing's eye, too. That's when he grew concerned. Whatever this musky-smelling creature was, it wanted to kill him badly.

This was no illusionary thing. It was real. It had probably been bound by Xaffer to this spell, which meant that Jenka had been transported to it, or the other way around. He couldn't concern himself with whys or hows now, though, for the beast was coming in again.

It turned its head one way, then another, and shook its gruff. The gesture was quite similar to a dog shaking off water, only this thing could bite a dog in half. Its first steps were misleading, for it was far quicker than it seemed. It lunged forward like a mouser on a rat. Its head came in straight at him, forcing him to choose a side to roll to. There was no time for deception, and the instant he committed to the left, the creature was there.

Claws met Dour-saturated flesh, and the radiant power saved him from being ripped to ribbons, but it didn't save him from having four claws rake across his skin. The pain kept Jenka from blasting at the thing, for he needed concentration to do that. Instead, he jabbed with his sword, forcing it to sidestep around him.

A few moments of circling, followed by a heartbeat of watching the thing's sheer frustration, and then it came at him again. Jenka had to jump up to avoid a set of finger-length clacking teeth. He ended up in a bad position and was forced to land in a heap on top of the creature's body.

It roared out and threw its neck back. Jenka went over it backward and was greeted with a hard thumping from its tail. One of the tail spikes punctured his shoulder, and when the beast turned, it stayed stuck in him, whipping him around to the floor, before coming free.

Jenka tried to roll away as it pounced on him, but he wasn't fast enough. He was pinned beneath two clawed forelimbs. A slavering snout opened as it made to eat his face. Jenka tried to roll away again, but it was wasted effort. Hot, rotten-smelling breath found his nostrils and threatened to make him gag, but he fought the urge. He reached deep into the Dour and did the one thing he hated to do most, and teleported himself away.

He didn't go far, but far enough to avoid those teeth was all he'd needed. He was fifteen paces away now and struggling to get to his feet.

The beast's mouth closed on air, and as it raised its head up to roar in confusion it saw him. It didn't wait. It charged straight in again, but this time Jenka had an idea of what to do.

As it closed the distance between them, Jenka feinted like he was diving to the left again. As soon as it leaned its bulk that way, Jenka spun the other direction and then pushed his sword deep into the monster's vitals, just behind the foreleg.

It roared out in pain and then went into a violent series of death throes, but by the time they subsided Jenka had found another brightly-painted red door set into the wall.

He didn't even bother to wipe the gore from his blade before he shouldered through it.

* * *

Marcherion sensed something behind them, or rather Blaze sensed it and Marcherion just felt it through their link. He looked over his shoulder and saw a dark thing not far behind. It was oozing through the air, not flying. On a second glance he couldn't spot it, but saw out of the corner of his eye another form revealed. He almost laughed at the idea of it. Some of those witches who had attacked the stronghold were following him.

Put them behind us, Blaze, March said, knowing his wyrm could fly three times as fast as he was now.

Nooo, Blaze responded. *There is another behind them. Aikira and the old wyrm.*

He was just about to have Blaze circle back when Aikira called out to him.

There is a faster way, she said, her tone and phrasing somehow pleasingly melodic to his ears. *Golden knows a way.*

She is ancient, she may, Blaze told March.

Be wary. There are some of those witches about, Marcherion warned. Blaze slowed down and circled once so that Golden could catch up to them.

"A way to what?" he called over to Aikira when they were close, glad to speak out loud. He and Blaze had once flown for more than a hundred days without communication by voice. March would just as soon speak out loud all the time.

"A *way*, a portal spell, or whatever it is." Aikira clearly didn't understand what it was. "If Crimzon and Jenka had only asked, she might have saved them the fli—"

Blaze hissed. *We only knowss where they are becausssse we can senssse Crimzon.*

And you will feed that destination into the weaving of the portal as I cast it into being, Golden joined the conversation. Her elderly ethereal voice was anything but matronly. She sounded as if she were taking control of the situation, though.

Marcherion didn't argue. If they could get there faster with a spell, then so be it.

CHAPTER NINE

"All this fargin' magic creeps my crotch," said Herald Kaljatig, High Commander of the Keepers. He wasn't very pleased with the new name chosen for his King's Rangers, but he couldn't argue with the idea that they no longer served "The Kingdom" and needed a new designation. He also hated the idea of magic, and the great hall Zahrellion had him investigating stunk of the arcane.

This was not the mildly upsetting, good kind of wizardry the Dragoneers and dragons used, either. This stuff was foul. This was the thick, blood-curdling type of witchery that Mysterian and those druids of Dou had thrown around, the kind Gravelbone and those fargin' Sarax used.

Herald wanted nothing more than to be out of there. Just being in the room made his missing eyeball itch. It was all he could do to keep from rubbing at the patch that covered the empty socket. It was only his fierce sense of duty that kept him at it.

Jenka had healed him, practically saved him from death, before he ran off. Herald hobbled on a cane these days when he was feeling spry enough to get out of the rolling chair Rikky had made for him. Today was one of those days.

"Herald, um, High Commander, I mean." Rikky's over-achieving attempt at being official was comical. He was trying to heal his pride, and Herald, understanding that, was humoring him. Seeing Rikky in his chair was disheartening. The boy usually had his peg leg on and was hopping around like the youthful man he really was. He'd crashed his dragon into an orchard, Herald had heard, or a group of ogres or something. Zahrellion said Rikky's stump was purple and far too sore to wear his peg. He was rolling across the floor expertly, though, looking in his lap at notes he'd jotted in a journal. "Do we believe the man was, well, a man?"

Herald looked at Rikky and shook his head. What was this *do we believe* stuff?

"We believe that men have to know about it, boy." Herald was losing his grip and tried not to snap too hard at the youngest Dragoneer. "We need to be shaking folks down on the other side of the wall. We need a ten-man… no twelve-man delegation to go over there and root these fargin' troll turds right outta their arse holes. We need to—"

Rikky's sudden burst of giggling laughter made it hard for Herald to continue. "Did you say root those troll turds right out of their arse holes?"

"It's an expression, boy," Herald defended, trying to remain deadpanned.

"'Root those rats out of their hidey-holes' is the expression." Rikky was still giggling.

Herald was glad to see it. The boy hadn't been himself since Silva was wounded and Marcherion and Aikira flew off without him. They'd been gone barely a full day and Zahrellion had ordered him and Rikky to find the witches' coven and bring them to justice. She and Lemmy were packing everything into Crystal's riding saddle in preparation for their departure to Clover's castle, where her son would be safe. Herald was glad for that, too. If he weren't standing beside a thick, dark puddle of goo that may or may not have once been a man, he might have felt great.

"Just an expression, boy," Herald repeated. He'd spotted a lump of cloth just under an overturned pew and started for it.

"It's a doll," Rikky said. His mirth faded, and he put his quill between his teeth so he could use his well-muscled arms to direct his rolling chair in that direction. "The witch came into the hall as a small girl."

Herald was leaning down to grab the raggedy thing.

"It may be magicked," Rikky said quickly. "If it is, it'll do more than creep your crotch, I'd wager."

Herald stopped mid-grab and backed away. He'd had the hair shocked off his nards by a Sarax once. He had no desire to feel anything like that ever again. "Why didn't you point it out, lad?" He cringed and hobbled a few steps back. "It almost got me."

Rikky was laughing now. He rolled over to the end of the pew and motioned for Herald to come help. Herald in turn motioned for one of the Keepers standing at the door to come do the lifting.

Once the pews were spread apart far enough for Rikky to roll his chair in, he went over to the doll and jabbed it with his quill.

"AAAAAAHHHHHHHGGGGGHHHH!" Rikky screamed and started waving his arms around crazily. Herald jumped back and must have had a terrified expression on his face for Rikky was holding his gut laughing at him now.

"Why do you want to send me to my grave, boy?" Herald asked after he'd gathered himself.

"Not your grave, to Mainsted." Rikky was looking at the doll again. His mirth evaporated as quickly as it had formed. "I saw these dolls in a shop there. It was not long before Zahrellion and I slew the serpent. I'm certain the place is still there."

"I'll order up a wagon team and have some mounted men start gearing up to escort us," Herald said.

"No. You and I will fly on Silva's back. We have men loyal to the Rangers and Dragoneers there. We saved them from Gravelbone's poison, after all."

What Rikky said next didn't do much to quell Herald's fear of riding on a dragon's back, but it eased most of the concern Herald had been feeling about the current situation.

"It's best that it was me and Zahrellion who stayed here," Rikky told him. "She and I have been through a lot. It's best that it is March responding to Crimzon's call as well. He and Blaze flew halfway across the world to join the battle against the thing we defeated. My pride will recover, and they are suited for it. It is Aikira that we should be worried about. I think she probably went to the Outlands, but she may have followed after March."

"Golden is the oldest of the wyrms," Herald said. "Those two will be fine."

Zahrellion stepped between the Keepers at the door, and after two dignified strides into the hall her face scrunched up and she ran like a terrified girl with tears streaming down her cheeks.

"What have I done?" she sobbed as she hugged Herald tightly. Then she was holding Rikky's head against her bosom, using the frame of his chair to keep herself upright. "I talked to her so terribly. I'm too horrible a person to be a queen. All I care about is keeping my son safe. I… I…"

"It's all right, lass." Herald gave her a hug. "Give her time. She will forgive you, I'm sure of it."

"I wish Jenka was here," Rikky blurted, before thinking.

Herald sighed. He hated crying girls almost as much as he hated magic and riding on dragons. Zahrellion was like a daughter to him now, though, and Rikky's comment had turned her into a sobbing mess of emotion. He stood there holding her until she was finished. It was the least he could do for the terrified girl.

CHAPTER TEN

Jade, Jenka's mental voice called out calmly. *I am in some sort of hedge maze now. This may take longer than I expected.*

Esssss. Jade showed in his tone that he wasn't pleased with this. *Sssshould I grow old waiting on you, like Crimzonssss for Cloversss?*

If you did, I'd hope we'd have friends as loyal as we are to come try to undo the magic keeping us apart. Jenka's ethereal voice revealed displeasure as well.

Yesss, Jade hissed an exasperated agreement. *I shall feed on the mackerels schooling off of the coassst here while I wait, then.*

You can't be hungry again already, Jenka laughed. It was the first time he'd done so in what seemed like ages, and Jade was pleased to hear it. *You just filled your belly with seals two days ago.*

Four dayss ago, Jade corrected. *We left the fire wyrm four dayss ago.*

Promise me that, no matter where you feed, you will return here to laze? Jenka asked.

Yessss, I wills. I will be here with you, Jenka. I am always with you.

With that, Jade leapt into the dusky sky and started winging his way toward one of the offshore reefs he'd found when flying high above the temple. Jade had seen larger fish gathering near the surface there and had been thinking of them ever since. When he saw the reef again, he grew excited. Toothy maw salivating for fresh meat, he banked around ever so slowly, searching the surface for a meal.

It was windy, and the clear water they'd seen before was choppy now. Where the swells rolled over the reef, they turned into huge, curling waves. These were far larger than the waves that ended on the rocky prominence where Jenka was.

It took a long time to spot a fish, but when he did, Jade was enthralled. It was perfectly sized. Small enough for him to lift from the water and large enough to be a tasty, juicy morsel.

Jade set his wings back and dove on the shadowy form that was now easing back into the deep.

He came down far harder than he normally would have, knowing that if he misjudged, water would be welcoming where earth was not. At the last second he leveled out and skimmed the wave tops, then he extended his long hind claws into the water and gripped the fish tightly. Trying desperately not to lose his forward momentum, he lifted his catch from the sea and found that it cost him a tremendous amount of energy just to carry it. He managed to rise and get going back toward the temple, but it was laborious at best. Then the long, slippery thing started wiggling frantically. First one claw lost its grip, then the fish was tumbling, only to splash into the sea and disappear in a swirling cloud of pink, bloody water.

Jade was almost relieved at not having the burden, but he was twice as hungry now as before, having worked up his appetite. He felt a surge of luck as the fish bobbed to the surface a good distance down current. He glided over that direction, hoping to snatch up the thing now that it wasn't moving, but he found that only the front half of his prey was there. Something must have eaten the tail end of it. The idea that something down there was big enough to take a bite out of him caused some of the gnawing in his belly to lessen, but only a fraction. He knew he could go check in on Crimzon and sate himself on plump sea lions. He would try to catch another fish first, this time one not so large as to be unmanageable.

After all, he had nothing better to do while waiting on his bond-mate to traverse the wizard's pitfalls.

* * *

Jenka fought the nausea that consumed him when he used the Dour. He levitated so that he could see the whole of the maze from a bird's eye view, and since he was used to flying, he found it wasn't hard to will himself to glide a few feet over the head-high growth.

The shrubs were thick, and the leaves had sharp little points on them. He'd tried dragging his hand on them, but the prickly stuff tore at his flesh. He then tried to hack through it with his blade, but that only frustrated him further. He decided that there might be a time when he had no choice but to ride the roaring flow of power, and maybe using the Dour a few times would better prepare him. Jade was probably right, but he disliked the unsettling roil the stuff left inside him. Feeling it now, as he hovered, had him questioning if he'd just rather wander around in the lanes below.

There was a fountained courtyard at the center of the misleading complexity of ever-branching pathways. It looked like three leaping fish all holding up a platter where a mermaid spat water in a steady stream. The spray fell back on her human breasts and cascaded down the rest of her fishy form like trickling jewels.

He shook his head, remembering to breathe, and thought of Zahrellion then. He missed her so much. He wanted this over and done with. He was a father. Well, he was supposed to be. He didn't even know if it was a girl or a boy, or what its name was.

It, ughhh, he growled into the ethereal. *I want to know. I need her.*

Yesss, Jade responded. *I am contemplatingss going to feeds with Crimzonsss.*

Sorry, I was thinking aloud, Jenka said. *I am levitating with the Dour now. You'd be proud.*

Yesss, but don't drift your mind ssso much. Keeps within yourself.

Yesss, Jenka responded and chuckled as he heard himself sounding like his bond-mate again. He could also feel Jade's hunger. *Go feed with*

Crimzon, but return before you laze. I may need you soon enough.

Yesss, Jade hissed, and then Jenka felt him divert his concentration as he leapt from his perch. He would be thinking of food until he fed. Such was the nature of the young, growing dragon.

Jenka had to force another dreamy vision of Zahrellion away from his mind. He couldn't lose himself again. He was very near the fountained courtyard now and made sure not to let the glittering water transfix his imagination again, too. He diverted his eyes as he let loose of the levitation spell and landed on the pavestones. He saw from the very corners of his vision the true nature of what was beneath him then, and he knew he'd made a mistake.

He was falling. The illusion would have tricked him even had he been walking, for where the pavestones radiated out from the illusionary fountain there was really nothing but a pit. Luckily it wasn't that deep, maybe twice as a man is tall. It was another battleground, and by the musty, briny way the place smelled he figured it was actually part of the temple's underground structure.

He landed hard on a dirty paved floor, then he began looking around. The only feature of the large rectangular room was a sizable waist-high block of stone at either end. He remembered seeing a similar sacrificial altar at the temple of Dou.

The stone nearest him was stained with blood and gore. All around it lay the decayed skeletons of larger things, some with horns and teeth, some more human than was comfortable to think about due to their great size. Behind each opposing altar block was a sizable barred gate, which probably cranked upward.

"My grandfather's trap actually caught one of you," the voice of a young man said from somewhere above him.

Jenka found it. It belonged to a dark-headed youth of about twenty years or so. The boy had a seasoned look about him, and his angled brow and deep, diving widow's peak left him looking far more sinister than Jenka imagined he could be. The high-collared sapphire-blue robe he wore looked like true wizard's garb, not something a priest or monk would wear.

"Well, then, if you're not just going to change into dragon form and slay us, we will complete Grandfather's rendering and dig out his journals for the rest of it." The young man looked up, and Jenka saw that a few others, these men robed in olive- and gray-colored robes, were starting to peer down from balconies set in the walls on either side of the pit. The top of the chamber looked as if it opened on the heavens themselves, but Jenka decided it was stained glass depictions and downward-facing mirrors that caused the effect. The concentrated illumination served to light up most of the fighting area. Jenka figured that he was a few stories under the tower of the newer temple now.

The sound of a chain rattling, and then the grind of metal sliding on metal came to his ears. He turned to see a twelve-foot-tall minotaur step out of the far gate's portal and start stretching its huge human arms and shoulders. Its horns were easily three strides wide, and its bullish head boasted two cherry eyes as evil as anything Jenka had ever imagined.

Jenka tested his grip on his sword, but decided then and there that this was when he needed to use the Dour most. He called out to Jade when the magic started filling him. He was consumed in the torrential rush of it, and briefly forgot himself. It was in this instant that he realized Jade wasn't responding to him.

Jade, he yelled again with his mind, but there was still no reply. After a third try, he knew no response was coming, and he readied his head for battle.

CHAPTER ELEVEN

The minotaur jumped over the altar and took two long strides before Jenka threw forth a fist of energy at it. It went staggering back and fell over the raised block. Then Jenka threw another blast upward at the green- and gray-robed men huddled on the balconies. The Dour inside him naturally shielded him from a sizzling streak of blue energy that came from Xaffer's grandson.

He disregarded the young spell-caster and continued focusing his concentration on the horned beast and his unresponsive dragon.

The minotaur jumped up onto the stone altar then and roared out as it flexed its muscles in a rage. Jenka decided to cast a levitation spell on his bullheaded foe and began to lift it from the altar.

The surprised creature waved its arms and legs around frantically while howling out its displeasure. Then Jenka wound his arm back as if he were throwing a ball and literally heaved the minotaur back into the hole from which it came.

He then reached out to Jade one last time before focusing all his power on the wizard.

Halfway through his call, his ethereal voice vanished completely. He heard the wizard laugh and knew he was completely alone now. No bond-link, no ethereal. It was a shame, he decided as he unleashed a flow of searing Dour on them all. This arena was large enough that Jade could have torn the roof right off of the new temple and flown in to join him.

"All we need is your blood, fool!" the young wizard called down with an authority surprising for his age. "Let us have some and we will let you leave. Refuse and we will draw it from your corpse."

Just then a whooshing of air behind Jenka caused him to dive and roll. Knives were flying, and from more than one direction. Most of the hurled objects were diverted from him by the natural aura of Dour protecting its host, but when a handful of men wearing uniforms, with swords and streamlined shields, rushed him, one of them finally found his flesh.

A dozen of the uniformed men were tackling him then, trying to get the blood from his new wound. In a rage, he squeezed himself together tightly.

"He is turning!" he heard one yell in anticipation.

"I've got a vial full, Xerrin Fyl," another man called before going into a fit of coughing.

"End it then," said the wizard.

Jenka let his body and his energy explode outward and men went flying away from him. One impacted the altar behind him so hard that the sound of his crunching bones cut above the din. Another's scream could be heard as a man sailed in an arc across the arena. It ended with a muffled thud.

Xerrin Fyl looked around at the amount of damage done to the arena and then pointed at the minotaur. "You! End this thing," he snarled and threw his arm forth. A flow of air-bending energy carried almost invisibly over into the creature.

The thing staggered and took a deep breath, then roared out with ten times the vigor it had shown earlier. It was growing, too. By the time it was across the space and on Jenka, it was twenty feet tall and literally raring to attack him.

Jenka wasn't sure how he was going to deal with such a thing. He would be easy prey for the wizard and his minions while he battled it; nevertheless he had to do something.

He turned and let five tiny streaks of intense Dour fly at the wizard called Xerrin Fyl, then teleported himself to a point in the air a few feet before the remaining two olive- and grey-robed men watching from the balcony.

With two quick jabs of his sword he opened their throats. They didn't even have a chance to register what was happening to them as blood spilled down their chests, and they went choking to the floor. A heartbeat later, Jenka teleported over to the young wizard.

Xerrin Fyl was ready. One of Jenka's little streaks of energy had found him and he didn't look pleased to have been scorched so easily. A shielding came flaring forth, burning Jenka's eyes and forcing his levitating body to tumble over backward and down. He caught himself before he crashed into the floor, but the minotaur was there. Jenka rolled over as the huge thing made to stomp him into the pavestones.

The whole arena trembled as the huge foot smashed down. A long moment of silence passed before the monster lifted it. At the same moment the minotaur let out a howl of frustration, Xerrin Fyl started cursing. There was no gooey mess underneath as they'd hoped.

The minotaur stopped raging and looked at its master curiously. It followed the wizard's eyes to its own chest, where Jenka had appeared knee-deep and was now kicking savagely into the creature's insides.

"If he's no dragon, he is as crafty as they come," Xerrin Fyl called up, but found that all of the balconies were empty.

The minotaur's heart was now a ruin. The monster fell forward, forcing Jenka to teleport yet again. This time he appeared on the balcony directly across from the wizard.

"You've a statue of a woman somewhere in this place. I will have it or I will destroy all of this."

"That bitch killed six of my grandfather's beasts before he contained her, and you are about to join her for all eternity, dragon." The smug look on the wizard's face told Jenka that men were coming up behind him. He started to turn to fight them, but a jolt of negative energy cut through him like an ax blow, leaving him incoherent and vomiting on the floor.

CHAPTER TWELVE

"This flying is for the fargin' birds, boy," Herald growled from behind Rikky. "These feet were never meant to leave the ground."

"Flying is for more than birds," Rikky laughed at the old ranger's discomfort. "We can land outside of Midwal for a spell, if you'd like. I'd hate for you to shit your britches up here."

"Nah, nah, lad. I'll stay put until we reach Mainsted. Just tell this wyrm to hurry it along."

"Remember you asked us to take it easy." Rikky sent Silva a mental command to make haste.

"Aye, I did, Rik," Herald grumbled. "But that was afore my legs were being stretched in twain over Silva's neck. I only have half an arse you— you— Oh, by the hells, what is she doing?"

"We are hurrying it along." Rikky wasn't sure Herald could hear him now over the wind, but by the way the old man was squeezing onto him, it was clear he was determined to get the ride over with.

Of all the Dragoneer wyrms, Silva was the fastest. She flew in an undulating flow that minimized her movements and propelled them in the air almost as if they were swimming through it. Within the span of a few heartbeats the world below was rushing past them in a blurry whir.

Rikky could hear Herald grumbling about his eyepatch almost blowing off or something but ignored it until they were within sight of Mainsted's harbor. When he heard, he wished he had paid attention.

"I almost lost my patch, and your chair tumbled off, boy. The lashings broke clean away."

"I've got my peg." Rikky's stump was bruised and sore, but no more so than the weeks right after his amputation, when he was forced to adapt or be swallowed by Gravelbone's invading horde. King Richard, Prince Richard then, riding his majestic blue dragon, Royal, saved him once out here. Now Richard rode the Nightshade and seemed unconcerned with the people struggling on the mainland.

As they glided over Mainsted's wall, Rikky decided he was wrong. These people were not struggling so much. The harbor was full of ships laden with goods. The streets were busy with commerce. Sure, some families were faring better than others, but that was the way of things.

"Might have gone to Midwal instead, Rik," Herald said. He was clinging to Rikky as if they were still flying fast. "Don't look like any witches have been causing trouble here."

"What would trouble caused by witches look like from up here?" Rikky asked. "Look at that there."

Rikky pointed down at someone who was jumping around and waving his arms.

The man went running through the cobbles to stay in sight of them. He knocked over an apple cart and forced a row of hooded priests to squeeze tight against a wall. He then ran up a ladder to one of the lower rooftops, snatching a length of brightly dyed material as he went. He finally stopped running and began waving the material around as if it were a flag. He pointed up to them and then to the roof of one of the taller structures. Rikky waved back and sent Silva in a slow circle around the place, allowing the eager person to climb the stairs up to the bell tower's balcony.

It took a while, but a man sporting a thick, well-trimmed beard appeared at the railing skirting the bell housing. He heaved spittle and air in and out of his lungs while holding a hand out, indicating that he needed a moment. After Silva hovered in as close as she could manage, Rikky realized he knew this person.

"What is your name?" Rikky asked. "I know you."

"You do." The man coughed but was getting his wind back. "You've a good eye, lad, for I've not recognized myself since I jumped the king in the harbor."

"Linux?" Rikky asked and felt Herald let go of him so he could reach for his sword.

"You can't slice him from here, Herald," Rikky chuckled.

"Your beard and gut go far toward hiding Rolph's youth," Herald called. "Last we heard, you were Richard's pet wizard."

"I ran off." Rolph's unkempt head lolled in shame. "The king is gone off into the deep. He cares nothing for his kingdom… nothing."

Rikky and Herald bobbed up and down in short slight rises and falls as Silva kept them in a somewhat steady hover.

"I've been hiding here, trying to scrounge up enough coin to get safe passage to Three Forks. Being a pot scrubber in Mainsted is a better way to pass my years than having the king's favor on the islands." The distraught man shivered in disgust. "He had me do things to people for him, terrible things. He was ruined by the demon, Gravelbone. He savors watching innocents suffer, and he swears that their sacrifice is the only thing that keeps him and his hellborn beast from killing even more of them."

"Have you heard of the Coven Wisteria?" Rikky blurted, eager to change the subject.

"Have they sent you for me?" Linux looked around the sky as if Marcherion and Zahrellion might appear on their dragons at any moment and attack him. "No… They have killed the remaining Hazeltine and seek to destroy anyone who was ever affiliated with the druids of Dou or Mysterian's witches. They have traders behind them, some of them charmed, I'm certain, but where coins flow so do capable men. They'd kill me if they knew who I was."

At the mention of his dead love's name, Herald sighed and grunted. "They attacked Queen Zahrellion's court and tried to kill Prince Jericho."

When Rikky looked back at him, Herald was scratching his head. "Does Richard have men looking for you?" the old ranger finally asked.

"I am certain he does."

"Why are the city guards gathering down there?" Rikky asked after Silva told him what she was seeing. Rikky saw that they had a dragon gun rolling in on a horse-drawn cart and heeled Silva around to go confront them.

Several of them had crossbows drawn and aimed, but none loosed when Silva stalled into a hover a few dozen yards above them.

"How dare you ready to fire on me and Silva!" Rikky said. "Who gave such an order, and who is so forgetful to obey?"

"I… uh… we follow Commander Fedran's orders," the man stammered. "He told us to warn you from the city, not to harm you."

"This city remains because of the Dragoneers, yet you would scare us from the sky?"

"I… uh… we… we are just following the orders we were given."

"Who tells this Commander Fedran what to do?" Herald asked sharply. "I'll nick the ear of any of you bastards that don't let the cat out of the sack."

The sergeant of the troop reached to his left ear. "Sir, I served with you at Kingsman's Keep before the Goblin King came."

The man looked even more afraid than he had been, as if standing before ear-nicking Herald was worse than standing before a silver dragon and its magic-wielding rider. "The commander orders us of his own will, but we all think his lover has gained more control of things than is proper."

"His lover?" Herald asked.

"What does she look like?" Rikky asked over them. "Is she beautiful? Is her hair long and silky black?"

Several men in the group nodded. All but one of them lowered their crossbows. Rikky marked the bolt still trained on them and decided that they'd better help Linux get out of the city and come up with a plan. This might be bigger than any of them expected.

CHAPTER THIRTEEN

Crimzon was full again and lazing. What little sky he could see outside the cavern was quickly turning from blue to gray. The waves crashing in had tripled in size, and even on the elevated shelf he'd claimed for a bed, tiny droplets of sea spray landed on his scales and sizzled away into a briny cloud of steam. It was from this somewhat hidden position that Crimzon learned the cavern had been marked as a feeding ground for something else.

He raised his head ever so slowly to get a good vantage and had to fight back his territorial instinct to keep from attacking. First one, then two tentacles snaked out of the deeper water near the opening. They moved expertly, and soon each snatched up a wriggling seal and slowly pulled away. The sea cows and rock lions were screaming as they did when he was feeding, each trying to warn the other that death was among them. Crimzon couldn't understand the creatures. The call they were making was clearly a warning, but not a single one of them tried to escape.

If only deer were so easy, Crimzon chuckled and let his concern over the thing feeding below slide away. Two of those juicy morsels would sustain any sizable creature for a while. He'd eaten eleven of them this time, which was just one more than his last feeding.

A few hours later the sky was black and Crimzon was seeing with his heat vision. Being a fire wyrm, sensing heat and cold was second nature to him. On the rocks and in the parts of the shallows where the sea wasn't crashing, long oval blobs of orange were piled here and there. The cooler rocks were deep blue, while the water was black. He was looking down and contemplating the idea that a fish in cool water would have to be the same temperature as the water it was in, or very close.

No, thatsss not ssso, he thought again. *When I go insss the water my scales do not cool.*

He saw another tentacle then, similar to the first pair. This one was a long thick line that disappeared into the violently splashing black water. It took more time and singled out one of the larger blobs of heat.

This piqued Crimzon's curiosity, and he studied it intently. The thing had a row of saucer-sized, and eventually plate-sized, suction cups down its underside, but had no eyes or nostrils that he could discern. The previous tentacles had been the same, and he was starting to think this was the same creature. He scanned the dark area below the surface, where the tentacle disappeared, and couldn't figure out what the appendage was connected to. Then he saw another tentacle in the back of the cavern, wrapped around one of the rocks. It had looked like a pile of seals, but now that he was following it, he realized the thing controlling the tentacles was already inside the cavern with him.

Ooohh. He let his breath out and began drawing a fresh one. It was an octerror, or its kin. He and Clover had seen a ship taken down by an octerror in Harthgar's busiest harbor. That one had been bound to the harbor master's will by a sea witch. He used it to keep the captains and their crews in line. They said it had once reached five blocks into town to snatch a man who didn't pay his fees proper. Crimzon remembered then that Clover said it used telepathy to single out the person. It could see the man's face through the mind's eye of the people around him.

Crimzon wondered what this one sensed about him. If it was looking through the eyes of the sea cows, it was seeing—

He couldn't wonder anymore, for two tentacles were reaching for him. He knew he couldn't let them grab him because the bulk of the blobby, under-beaked thing would eat a few chunks before he could get away. What he needed to do was find the thing's eyes.

He pushed himself up to fly to a higher perch, but the effort resulted in nothing but pain and anger. He held back a roar of frustration, but only until one of the tentacles came close. He could see its bulk, half in, half out of the water, and backed tightly against the cavern wall.

The octerror had eight tentacles, he knew. He couldn't defend himself against even half of them at once. Inside of its reach was where he needed to be. It was the only place he had a chance against such a thing.

He leapt, right over the closing tentacle, seventy feet, and landed with his claws ankle-deep in the sloshing sea. He nearly landed on the suddenly alarmed beast. Steam exploded around him as he roared out and bathed the sea monster with his dragon fire.

In the stark illumination he saw its cold black eyes and knew the bright flames were hurting them. He managed to char to stiffness the point where two of the tentacles connected.

The sea cows, startled first by his leap, then by his roaring blast of flame, went mad with their warning calls. Crimzon was grateful, for the sudden mass of alarmed mental signals left the octerror momentarily stunned.

It was a devastating attack, but not enough to end the thing. As Crimzon drew a second breath, the octerror brought more of its tentacles to bear. It was using three of them to keep itself anchored and now the remaining three to swat and smash at Crimzon.

He ducked and dodged and was pummeled backward into the water. In half a second his lower legs and the stalk of his tail were wrapped. He thrashed and shook but couldn't get loose. He finished drawing air and then blasted his flames downward over the gripping tentacles, knowing that his scales kept him from burning himself. He cooked one of them, and the other withdrew, leaving him falling into the rocks.

Crimzon landed hard. Several of his huge rib bones took most of the impact. One of them broke from it, and though it wasn't a debilitating injury, it left him unable to fill his lungs at will.

He had to jump away, back to an elevated perch and gather himself. This was a formidable foe. It could kill him. Right now it was thrashing about in pain, trying to cool its burns in the sea water, but this wasn't over.

Once he was situated, Crimzon cast a minor spell of healing on his rib. He also surrounded himself with wards that rendered his psionic mind unreachable. Just for good measure, and a bit of a distraction, he formed a ball of fire in his front claws and slung it at the bulk of the sea monster. Then he drew in the deepest breath he could manage and leapt back down to finish the battle.

CHAPTER FOURTEEN

Underneath her calm and steady demeanor Zahrellion was a frantic mess. She was going mad. Her heart was so torn between the joy of motherhood, the nagging want for Jenka, and now fear for the safety of her son, that she was falling into a state of despair.

They'd just arrived at Clover's castle, and she found that no place should feel more like home than here. It was here she and Jenka had first made love. They'd conceived Jericho here. It was from here that the Dragoneers eventually triumphed over the druids and the freakish alien thing that had ensorcelled them. It was here she'd given birth to Jericho.

Empty, the place was like a tomb for sweet memories. Lemmy was here, and several of the ogres who helped tend the territory surrounding the protective field, but without the Dragoneers it wasn't quite home.

She gave Crystal instructions to return to Three Forks, where men were waiting to load her down with a larger harness rig so she could bring the things and few people Zahrellion needed to keep Jenka's kingdom from falling apart. And now that her wyrm was winging away she really started feeling alone.

Jericho, the one light in all the darkness and uncertainty, saved her with a giggling chirp from his crib. He would be hungry soon, and she was weaning him. There were peaches, lots of peaches, all gifted to them by some orchard owners. It seems the ogres the boys killed had been ravaging their trees for some time.

Zah was also furious that someone was bold enough to try to steal her son. She had a strong feeling that Richard was behind it somehow. He was the only person alive who was threatened by Jericho's existence. She understood that whoever raised Jericho was molding the future of the kingdom, so she tried to keep her ill emotions from showing as she put him to her breast.

When the baby was finished feeding, she put the crib just inside the door to Clover's private library. She then started going through the drawings and documents scattered there just to pass the time. There were several sketches of the Sarax, and Zah couldn't help but wonder if there were more of them in other parts of the world. She also found a sketch of Vax Noffa as a boy. She wondered what it was like for him being raised by a legendary dragon rider. She wondered what it was like for Aikira being raised by him. Like Vax, Jericho might be forced to live without the joy of a dragon bond. It pained her to think so, for the only two things that rivaled the love she felt for Crystal were her love for her son, and her love for Jenka.

Before long, she grew tired and took Jericho to the room she and Jenka shared. There the two of them slept, softly and soundly.

* * *

Lemmy was out gesturing with the ogres, telling them of happenings that concerned their kind. He told them they needed to round up the remaining ogres tainted by druid magic and end them. He warned they should do this before men started thinking they were all savage. Two of the ogres nodded understanding and loped off to spread the message, while the others just shook their heads in disgust. Then one of the younger males came forth and indicated that he wanted Lemmy to follow him. Of course, Lemmy did so.

They went down toward the cavern where the alien's craft was buried, but they didn't stop there. The ogre led Lemmy through that valley and up the far ridge. It was quick going as both of them moved through the mountains with animalistic grace. The ogre's dexterity was born from its strength and instinct; Lemmy's athleticism was born in the elven half of him.

Before long they were coming to another cavern, a smaller one that once housed a bear but was now the home of some younger ogres, probably including this one.

Once they were at the opening, a witchy-looking woman stepped out of the darkness. It wasn't the witch who had attacked in Three Forks, but by the markings on her robe, she was clearly one from the same coven.

Lemmy drew his sword and made to dart away but found two other witches closing in on him from behind. He spun, slicing a complete circle. He even jabbed the blade out at one of them but only got the tip tangled in an empty robe. Then a jolt hit him and his sword came free, but he was falling to the rocks. The blade clattered away and stopped, leaving a pristine ring hanging in the air.

When he moved his eyes upward, he saw himself standing there. The witch had transformed herself to look like him. Just like the one binding him with rope had made herself look like an ogre. He tried to struggle, but he was under some sort of spell that suppressed his ability to think clearly. His only thought was that he had to protect Jericho and warn Zah, but even that idea began to cloud and slip away from him. Then he was in a daze. A happy cheer settled over him and he found he had never been more content to stare at a cavern wall.

A day later, when a pair of dark wolves came sniffing around, they found him. Lemmy couldn't help but giggle with delight as they tore him apart and ate him.

* * *

Zahrellion woke to find Lemmy standing at the door. He was watching Jericho, as if the child fascinated him. This wasn't strange to her, because elves had a terribly slow reproductive rate. Children, childhood, and the whole birthing process were cherished. With Lemmy being half-elven, Zahrellion wasn't sure he could even reproduce. Oddly, this made her giggle, for the girls who attended her would be disappointed to learn such a thing. They all stared dreamily at him when they saw him. Every single one of them would have loved to bear his child.

The baby was standing in the crib now, using the side rails to keep himself upright, and Lemmy started over to protect him from the fall that was surely to come.

"He has to learn to fall down, too, Lem." She smiled, startling him. Apparently Lemmy hadn't known she was awake and eyeing him. He shook his head, as if waking from a dream.

For the fleetest of moments she felt fear for her son, but it passed when Crystal's roar echoed around the valley outside.

"Come, Jericho, Lemmy." She grabbed the baby into her arms and brushed past his golden-haired protector. "Let us see who and what actually made the journey."

Zahrellion was pleased that one of the brawny cooks and two of the braver girls had come. There were things to do to make the place suitable for raising Jericho, and having help would make it all the easier. What she didn't understand was the sour look on Lemmy's face as he took in the new arrivals.

CHAPTER FIFTEEN

"Do you know where they gather and plan?" Rikky asked Linux hopefully. It was Rolph's unshaven mug before him, but he never knew Rolph, so it was easier for him to think of the person wholly as Linux now.

"Oh, were it so easy, lad," Herald chimed in.

They were gathered in a huddle around a small blue druid's fire out beyond the city. A light drizzle was coming down. It was cold enough to see each other's breath, but not unbearable with the flames there to warm them.

I will feed, Silva told Rikky.

He nodded his response and she leapt into the darkening sky.

"They are secretive." Linux shrugged his shoulders. "And they aren't all as powerful as their leader. I would like to know from where she came, and how she gained her power, for it is considerable. I wonder was she a Hazeltine who rebelled, or just a pot wizard who chanced upon something powerful? *The Chronicles of Derralin* tell us that—"

"Bah! Enough with the druid speak," Herald barked. "What are you telling me?"

Linux looked at Rikky and chuckled. "I am saying that, if we get the leader, the rest will dissolve—uh—dissipate—uh—go away."

"I know what dissolve means, man," Herald grumbled. Then he looked up at Rikky, as if an idea had struck him. "All you need to catch a fish is bait and a basket." He looked at Linux now, who suddenly appeared uneasy. "They want to get rid of all you druidoos. They'll come for you, I'm sure of it. We can catch them, if we set a trap."

Linux looked at Rikky. Rikky narrowed his brows in a way that told Linux he agreed with the old ranger. "It's a good way for you to prove your loyalty."

"I guess it is," Linux nodded. "But how many know I am in this skin?"

"I'm not sure it will be enough to prove anything," Herald said. "You could easily have been sent here by Richard to take our measure. And if me and some men I know parade you through the city proclaiming that we have the king's absconded druidoo, they'll chance an attempt. That's when Rikky and his wyrm'll come swoopin' in and end 'em!" Herald grinned, as if it was a perfect plan.

Linux's tone was sarcastic when he spoke. "I planned on being in the streets of Mainsted at the perfect moment to meet you then, did I?"

"He couldn't have planned that, Herald," said Rikky. "He saw us and took a chance."

"Bah! He is a druid and could have pocussed himself right where we were, or some such. I don't know."

Rikky nodded, indicating that he wouldn't trust Linux so easily, and Herald let it go.

"Tell me you have food." This from Linux, who looked very hungry at that moment.

"We do." Rikky started to get up, but Linux went for the pack, saving Rikky from trying to stand with only one leg. Rikky couldn't forget the kindness and help Linux had given him after he'd lost his leg, but this was a different person. This was a different body anyway, with the soul of one who would end an innocent's life so he could cheat death.

"Herald's plan needs work," Linux said, his words still drenched in sarcasm.

"That was really a plan?" Rikky asked Herald, who reddened into a look that Rikky couldn't quite figure out.

After a meal of cheese, hard bread, and dried beef, Linux and Rikky whispered over Herald's snoring and started making a more intricate plan to catch the witch.

* * *

Crimzon twisted out of the octerror's tentacle and then spun on the rocks, catching the swinging appendage in his powerful jaws. The sea monster swung back around, lifting the giant dragon from his hind legs, but Crimzon didn't let go. Instead, he swung his bulk the other way and shook his head in a savage manner. The tentacle was nearly severed between his teeth, and he was forced to let go. He landed in the sloshing surf, and his heat sent steam billowing up around him. He darted one way, then changed direction in a disturbingly sinuous fashion that bewildered the thing just long enough. Crimzon came out of his own steam like a striking serpent and managed to blast a huge gout of fiery breath directly into one of the creature's eyes.

The octerror swung around again, its limp appendages following the motion like waterlogged ropes. Two of its four still-functioning tentacles latched onto rocks in a wide stance and the other two reached out for Crimzon in a closing motion that was sudden enough to block his instinctual leap for escape.

The big red wyrm did leap but didn't miss the wrapping tentacle that came around. His bulk carried him over onto the monster's soft, squishy bulk, and half of the cavern was splattered with a gushing squirt of dark, inky fluid.

In the illumination thrown by a lightning strike, Crimzon saw that the water had turned from scarlet to black. He felt himself being squeezed and knew that if he didn't draw in a breath he wouldn't be able to char his way out of the position he was in.

Now the thing was trying to squeeze out from under him and get its sharp beak through his scales and into his flesh. Wriggling and roaring, scratching and clawing as best as he could, Crimzon fought for enough room to get air into him. He fought with all he had. He managed a little and then spent it burning the limb that had hold of him.

The grip loosened and he gathered more breath. This time, as he let it loose, the thing squeezed even harder and brought its remaining free tentacle to bear.

Crimzon blasted at it, and blistered it raw, but the creature was determined. It shook the dragon and then started using its other tentacles to pull itself out of the cavern. Crimzon was being crushed. He had to clear his mind to cast a spell before he lost consciousness. When he finally finished his casting, his skin flashed white hot. The octerror let go of him. It was scalded by a pulse of energy hot enough to melt some of the rocks around them.

Crimzon's scales boiled the water, and he let out a savage roar.

The octerror had backed against the cavern wall and looked like it only wanted to flee now. It was scorched, sporting several deep, seeping burns. Crimzon circled around the thing, allowing it the opening, and as it slid back into the storm-raged sea he felt, more than saw, what was happening behind him.

Another octerror, half again as big as the one he'd just maimed, was there feeding on the smoldering sea-life available.

It stopped stuffing the fat, white, blubbery seal flesh into its ship's-bow-sized beak when it sensed Crimzon's gaze, but it didn't stop feeding. Secured in place by three of its tentacles, it kept feeding with most of them, but then absently swatted Crimzon against the wall with another.

The dragon impacted so hard he wasn't sure he would recover from the blow. It didn't matter, though. Already several more tentacles were wrapping around him. He roared out into the ethereal, but it was a feeble attempt. He craned his neck this way and that, trying to sink his teeth into something, but it never had the chance to happen. Another tentacle wrapped his head. His jaws slammed shut as it cinched down and squeezed him. Before long he couldn't even draw breath. He laughed inside, then, realizing that of all the deaths he had imagined over the centuries, he had never dreamed of being eaten by a creature of the sea.

CHAPTER SIXTEEN

"Why won't you transform for me?" Xerrin Fyl asked for the umpteenth time. "Did my grandfather leave a ward dangling over this place or something? If you only helped me finish his journey, I would let you loose."

"Are you talking to yourself?" Jenka's voice was hoarse, and he felt groggy at best, but the wizard had been talking for a long while, and he was tired of listening.

"You are conscious? Yes? Good." He gave a slight nod before continuing. He looked more curious than anything. "I am Xerrin Fyl, High Priest and Keeper of the Fyloch. Why didn't you turn into your dragon form and break away from us?"

"Because I am not a dragon."

Xerrin Fyl didn't like that response. He took a long stride and planted his hard, pointed boot tip soundly into Jenka's crotch. It was a debilitating blow. Jenka tried to back away but wrist and ankle manacles kept him from getting anywhere.

"You are a dragon," the young wizard snarled. "Only one of dragon blood could have passed through the second door and entered our arena." He put his hands behind his back and started pacing back and forth as he spoke. He wasn't old, but he had a definite aura of formidability about him. "The draconic glow of your eyes is all the proof I need. You are a green wyrm. Some of my men saw you in the sky the day before you came into grandfather's temple. Fishermen saw you flying overhead the day before that."

Jenka tried to sink into the Dour then. He found it was like sinking into an empty well of blackness. The cell must have been warded, or maybe the chains. He tried to reach out for Jade, too, but the lack of connection served only to dishearten him. He'd been in a dungeon before. He knew he was at this fool's mercy. If he wanted to see Zahrellion and his child, he would have to think his way through.

"I am a dragon rider," Jenka croaked. "My wyrm is still out there. If I do not return in three days, he will tear your temples to the ground."

"A sound threat." Xerrin Fyl nodded. "Only you've been here four days and he has not come raging in to save you." The wizard shook his head. "You say you seek the statue of the bitch my grandfather baited his trap with, and I am curious as to why?"

"Her name was Clover, and she was a dragon rider, too. Your grandfather was wrong." Jenka tried not to sound as if he were pleading, but the lack of Jade, and now the absence of all that Dour had him feeling more vulnerable and afraid by the moment. "Dragons cannot change into human form."

Xerrin Fyl considered the idea. "If you are just a dragon rider, I have no use for you." He squatted down just beyond the reach of Jenka's boot and looked him in the eye. "I will introduce you to Clover tonight. Fyloch willing, you will join her in petrification for eternity."

"Who is this Fyloch?"

"The most powerful god in all the universes," the wizard replied. A dreamy gaze passed across his eyes, as if thinking about Fyloch gave him pleasure. "I think he will enjoy you. He gives us glory for battling the darkest of things in our arena."

"Why not just let us go?" Jenka asked stupidly. The plea in his voice was undisguisable now, and it made Xerrin Fyl let out a snort of disgust.

"I am starting to believe you." The wizard stood. In a dramatic show of disrespect, he hawked and spat on Jenka. "No dragon would seem so cowardly. Fyloch may tire of you before the morrow comes."

* * *

In the illumination of a lightning flash, and through the slanting downpour of rain, Jade saw a pair of rock lions floating in the open sea. By the savage teeth marks on one of them, it was clear they were dead. Even as Jade studied them from the dark sky above, the body heat from a fish as long as a canoe, swimming faster than Jade could fly, shot through the water and devoured one of them.

As the formidable feeder disappeared down into the depths, Jade looked ahead and saw more dead sea-life from the cave. He wondered if Crimzon had gone mad and killed more than he could eat. No, Jade decided, mighty Crimzon could eat rock lions one after the other and probably never be fully sated.

Jade was worried for Jenka. Not feeling his bondmate there was like having a hole torn through his insides. He missed his rider and was certain that Jenka needed his strength to get through the old wizard's trickery. They hadn't even wondered what happened to the Soulstone Xaffer had used, and Jenka was likely to wind up sitting on the floor dreaming of Zahrellion for days on end. Jade had a bad feeling about it all, and these floating chunks of meat only served to make it worse.

He was hungry, and he planned to feed in the cavern, but he'd come for Crimzon's wisdom, too. The old fire drake would help him.

Jade's instinct to attack the temple and free his bond-mate was suppressed when he grew near the place. It was warded to repel his kind, but that spell could be broken. All he had to do was face the revulsion and crash through.

There will be a second spell released if you do that, Jade heard his mamra's voice speak in his head. *The second will stun you, trap you, or end you for good. Find another way.*

The knowledge she had filled him with as she lay dying came to him often. He let her voice guide him. That was the real reason he'd returned to the cave, because she would have told him to do so.

Jade could see the darkened entrance up ahead, and there were several more floating seals. There were more of the long feeders, too, eating them from underneath.

A growling, roaring sound forced itself through the noise of the stormy sea, and Jade looked to see a huge sea creature slinking out of the cavern mouth. Alarm washed over him like a tidal wave as he swept into the hole and saw another, larger, one about to bite into the limp red wyrm he revered so much. He instinctually lunged his head at the thing's eyes and let loose a blast of his hot, noxious spew. The octerror let Crimzon fall into the sloshing black water and made to swat Jade with a tentacle, but Jade dove under it and came down claws first right on the beast's blubbery bulk.

Within a matter of seconds Jade scratched a dozen deep furrows into the monster, but the thickness of its hide, and the slippery substance coating it, forced him to take back to the air.

Jade knew it was hurt. When the next lightning flash came from outside, he saw that at least one side of its bulk was covered in blood. One of its eyes was ruined, but it was still intent on eating Crimzon.

Jade was slammed then by an unseen limb, causing him to rake a wing on the cavern wall and tumble into the pink, frothy water. The next thing he knew, he was being pulled under. It all happened so fast he could barely blink. He tried to struggle, but a tentacle was wrapped around his neck and shoulders so tightly that he couldn't think. He saw, in a flash of lightning, Crimzon's huge body being bashed against the rocks over and over again. Then he was taken under.

CHAPTER SEVENTEEN

"What are they, again?" Rikky asked Herald and Linux.

They were in one of the three market squares inside the city walls of Mainsted, standing at the fringes of a crowd gathering around a person staked to a pole atop a pile of hay bales. They'd come to the square to use Linux as bait, but this scene was already unfolding when they arrived. Standing up on the first layer of bales was a trio of well-groomed men wearing cloaks as black as night. They had their hands on the hilts of their swords and seemed as if they'd have no hesitation making an example of the first person who grew unruly in the crowd.

"Grimwielders, lad. Shhh." Herald hushed him so he could hear what the leader was saying.

"Linux, what are Grimwielders?" Rikky persisted, noticing several other of the black-cloaked men guarding the pyre circle.

Herald glared at him, but Linux explained in a whisper that carried to Rikky in the ethereal.

They are a guild of thieves, assassins, and such. They've been around since the beginning, earning their coins in the shadows for whoever can afford their services. Mysterian once told Vax Noffa and me that the Hazeltine used them sometimes when they needed muscle. I know for certain King Blanchard used them. This is unusual, though, for they've never acted publicly before.

Rikky pulled on Linux's sleeve. Only when the High Master Druid met his gaze did he voice his mind. *I'll not let them burn that man. No matter what he did.*

Not even if he is a murderer or a rapist?

Not until he's been judged guilty of such a crime by his queen. Rikky's ethereal voice was firm.

We are not in the Frontier, Rikky. Zahrellion has no sway. Richard doesn't care, either. This is how justice is handled here now, though it does not appear that this gathering is about justice at all. Listen… they are saying that the man is a druid of Dou, that he was caught trying to buy menstrual rags to use in casting spells. He most certainly is no druid.

Rikky scrunched up his face but remembered Master Kember using the rags of village women to attract bucks during the rut. It seemed disgusting, but it was one of the best ways to draw in a big one. He listened to the Grimwielder's accusations and grew angrier by the moment. The man strapped to the pole was pleading for his life.

The Grimwielders jumped down and a whoosh erupted, sending smoke and sparks billowing up. The crowd all gasped and stepped back, save for Rikky, who was hobbling as fast as he could on his peg leg away from the gathering.

* * *

Linux watched Rikky go for a moment and then started forcing his way through the people toward the growing blaze. He grabbed Herald by the sleeve and pulled him. Another gasp was heard, but only from the few who had been looking away from the fire. Linux already knew the cause of it and kept moving toward the staked man.

"I've got three daughters," the man screamed. "PLEEEEAAAASSSE! Ah! Ah! I feel it!"

Herald apparently understood the situation, for Linux heard the ranger's steel ring free. Then Linux shouldered past the Grimwielder before him and unleashed a spell that suppressed the flames just long enough for Silva and Rikky to come swooping by and snatch the man, stake and all, from the middle of it.

The crowd was screaming then. The tight, empty circle of people was suddenly thrice its diameter, for here came Silva spewing forth a molten gout of liquid goo that hardened into a pewter-like metal over the extinguished blaze.

Herald and Linux ran to the edge of it, and Silva let the staked man down near them before stepping up onto his self-made pedestal. Linux began knifing the ropes loose with his dagger, while Herald stood over them.

Where the man had just been tied to a post and surrounded by flame, the silver dragon reared up and spread its wings in a show of sheer dominance. Even though he was on their side, Linux was terrified by this. She might be the smallest of the Dragoneer wyrms, but Silva was as powerful as any of them.

The roar that followed was thin, for it came from Rikky, not his dragon, yet it was no less fierce than Silva's call would have been.

Linux almost laughed at the boy.

Everyone was fleeing, save for the Grimwielders and a few old crones. For the span of half a heartbeat he found that curious, then Linux understood that they were the ones who had just been trapped. The crones all threw back their hoods at once and revealed their witchy youth. Worse, the man he had just untied was now the voluptuous Ankha Vira, infamously beautiful leader of the Coven Wisteria. She was licking her blood-red lips as she sank her bladed nails into his face with one hand and sent a pulse of sparkling lavender power at Rikky with the other.

Linux felt his cheeks ripping; he also felt Herald's boot kick the witch in the side of her head.

"Get on, you fat, fargin' frog-eatin' wench!" the ranger yelled.

The witch went rolling away as if she were a tumbleweed in a gale. She rolled thrice in the time a normal person could have rolled once, and she came up rubbing the bleeding knot Herald had given her. She looked as angry as any woman Linux had ever seen.

Silva blasted at Ankha Vira with her molten spew, but when it all settled the witch was gone. The Grimwielders and the other witches were still there, though, and they didn't appear to be fleeing.

The mercenaries' involvement in the mess became clearer as three of them moved around to the right. One of the witches had her hand out and was clearly controlling them with a spell. Another witch was forcing two of the men out before Silva, so that the dragon had to choose which group to face. It was clear that even though the two Grimwielders had their swords out and ready, they were terrified and looked to be fighting the will that was commanding them.

As Silva's head darted down toward the two men, Rikky surprised the witch controlling them by pummeling her with a blast of Dour magic from the dragon tear mounted in his bow. It surprised Linux, too, for he'd forgotten the boy had gathered one until that moment. When the witch's body impacted the ground, part of her was crushed into the cobbles. Her legs and lower torso were instantly little more than a pulpy stain, while the rest of her twisted apart and slid a few dozen paces.

When Rikky roared this time, Linux didn't even think of laughing. In fact, he found the look on the young man's twisted face quite disturbing.

Herald vomited, and the remaining two witches vanished in a flash. They must have let loose the spells holding the Grimwielders, for they were looking around with eyes full of fear and confusion now, too.

"Back to lookin' for them wicked bitches, I guess." Herald spat away some of his revulsion and took in the guildsmen around them.

"What do we do with them?" This came from Rikky.

"We know where they gather," one of the Grimwielders said quickly.

"They were bewitched," Linux said.

Rikky had Silva ease her head down toward the man who had spoken. "Tell us where they gather, then," he commanded.

The man told him as quickly as he could speak.

CHAPTER EIGHTEEN

Zahrellion could easily understand why Lemmy had no interest in hearing her complain about Aikira's absence, or how she was so sorry for berating her. No one wanted to listen to a woman ramble on and on. Zah's follies as Queen Regent, Dragoneer, and friend were none of his concern. She wasn't certain why he was keeping such a distance from the baby, though. Normally he gave Jericho his full attention. Many times in the past she had been amazed by Lem's interaction with the boy. The half-elf would spend hours exercising the baby's legs and arms with soft, gentle movements. He would put him in his lap, legs out, and place his palms on the baby's feet and move them as if Jericho were walking. Not only was it cute, but it would help the child's coordination immensely.

Lemmy had once written Zahrellion a note explaining that one of the reasons elves and half-elves were so dexterous was because their mothers did a whole lot more than just feed and ogle their get.

Zahrellion wondered what Lemmy thought about all the time. He never spoke aloud because he was a mute. On occasion they'd conversed in the ethereal, but not lately. He was so gorgeous that any girl would fall for him, but he'd never been all that interested in girls, as far as she could tell.

Jenka had told her that Lemmy's elven blood might kill a human girl if she conceived. He would live a longer life than most people and would hopefully find a girl of elven blood and help the race repopulate.

Lemmy didn't seem as pleased to be here as she thought he would be. In the past, Lemmy had loved the foothills and used to roam them with the rangers, and even the ogres, but for the last few days he'd done little more than prop himself against a wall and watch the baby.

His mood changed when Crystal came in from another supply flight from Three Forks. The dragon told Zahrellion that Rikky and Herald had found the Coven Wisteria and wanted Zah and Crystal to come help with the attack.

Of course, Zahrellion agreed.

Lemmy held the baby, rocking him like an experienced mother might to keep him still, while Zahrellion donned her Dragoneer armor and made ready.

"You'll feed him from the bladder? You'll keep him safe?" she asked as she prepared.

Lemmy nodded that he would, and she felt as sure as a mother could that her son, Jenka's son, would be safe while she was gone.

Zah kissed Jericho's pink forehead and gave some instructions to the ogres who tended the lands around the castle. After that she ran the stairs up to the dragon landings, climbed onto Crystal's back, and took to the air, flying south as fast as her frigid wyrm could go.

The wind was refreshing and helped, at least for a while, to clear her worries away. She looked forward to wreaking her vengeance on the haughty witch who'd dared to try to steal her child. Then thoughts of Jenka assailed her, and sadness took over again. There were no words for how much she missed him.

* * *

Jenka saw her. Crimzon was right. Even still, she was as fierce-looking and beautiful as a woman could be. Just looking at her made his heart race with something akin to fear, yet tinged with more than a little desire. She didn't look to have actually been turned to stone. Her skin still retained a peachy color, and her hair was as red as any he'd ever seen. She looked as if she'd been about to clobber someone with a spell, the final words of the casting frozen on her lips.

Jenka was suspended by his arms between two robed men, his limp form dragging roughly behind them. When he wouldn't turn into a dragon, Xerrin Fyl blasted him with some powerful stunning spell. His bones felt as if they'd been liquefied, but they hadn't—at least he hoped not. According to the murmuring between the acolytes, he was about to be solidified, just as Clover had been.

He was too weak to struggle, and he'd called to his dragon so hard in the ethereal that his mind was worn out. He could do little more than watch as he was seated on a stool and leaned back against a wall for support. Unlike Clover, who looked to be in mid-stride toward whomever she was attacking, he was doomed to spend eternity in some awkward and uncomfortable position.

"You've had your last chance," Xerrin Fyl said from the damp doorway. "You wanted to find the statue of the dragon rider my grandfather tricked. Well, here she is. Make a prayer to your gods, for the time has come for you to join her."

The room had to be below the level of the sea, for Jenka had been dragged down several more flights of stairs. He reached for the Dour of the teardrop mounted in his sword and could feel it, but it was in the pile one of the acolytes had dropped in the corner near his armor. Its power didn't respond to him. Nor did the power from Clover's teardrop, which was in the pouch tied to his sword belt. Jenka tried to sink into the Dour that was flowing through him as well, but the wards on the structure kept the power from serving him.

At that moment he found he longed for the sickly feeling caused by teleporting with Dour. He might have been able to stand and stagger to Clover's form and then teleport them away, but the Dour wasn't there for him. Knowing that he had let down Zahrellion and his child and the other Dragoneers was hard to bear. Knowing he'd let down Crimzon, and now Clover, too, was enough to make him break.

Xerrin Fyl laughed, and his followers sneered and chuckled along with him; then he stepped over and cast a spell that made Jenka feel as if he'd been frozen from the inside out. Vision left him and sound soon followed. His need to draw breath vanished, as did his sense of touch. Within minutes he was stiff and solid, yet semi-conscious of what was going on around him.

The sea of Dour he usually sank into was now an ocean of despair. He missed Zahrellion; he missed his dragon even more. Then the full sense of doom, the idea that he couldn't get out of here and see any of them ever again, started taking over. This wasn't a dungeon that he could eventually leave. He'd been spelled still, and would remain so for all eternity.

Worse, Jade would come to rescue him and be trapped. The poor wyrm would be chained in the arena to fight the summoned beasts Xerrin Fyl and his cronies favored.

It amazed Jenka how unafraid he was for himself. After a while, his sense of failure grew so strong it drowned out all else.

He tried to think about Zahrellion, but her image wouldn't form in his mind's eye. This saddened him to the point of breaking yet again, and had he been able, he would have bawled like an abandoned babe.

PART III
INTO THE STORM

CHAPTER NINETEEN

"Are you there, boy?" a soft voice asked. "Hello?"

Suddenly, Jenka felt a presence beside him. Crimzon had said there would be a demon or demi-god bound to the wizard's more powerful castings, and Jenka suspected that this was it. He tried to turn and look but couldn't move. Nor could he use his eyes in any normal sense.

"Yes, that's it," the decidedly feminine voice said. "A young man, nonetheless. Lucky me."

A form, one that was more of a projection into his mind than a reality, appeared, stepping in front of Jenka. He knew at once it was Clover. She was every bit as beautiful as Crimzon had described. She was long and lithe, and so perfectly rounded at the breast and hip that Jenka found himself unable to think. Her lips were full and wet, and her hair was like blood flowing over her shoulders.

"You have to tear away from the spell, man," Clover said, running the back of her hand down his abdomen until it found his crotch. There she kneeled in front of him and cupped him. A grin slowly crept across her face. Then she rolled her shoulders, and closed her eyes dreamily. "Once you do, I'll make you forget the pain."

"How do—?" he tried to ask, but no sound came.

"Shhhhh," she hissed, touching his nose with the same finger she shushed him with. "I can't hear you until you tear away from the spell. Your physical body will still be where it is, but your consciousness will be free to roam this empty plane with me and keep me company. And I do need some company, boy. I don't even know how many decades I've been here."

Jenka tried to lean his head forward and pull from the stillness but couldn't move. He tried clenching his body and limbs. He tried swinging an arm and pulling in his knees, but nothing happened. While he was struggling to grasp the situation, Clover was caressing his hardened skin and subtly pleasuring herself. It was very distracting, to say the least, and had he not been spelled, he doubted he could resist her.

She was breathtaking to behold, with leather armaments that fit her form perfectly, and hips that ground against his thigh. Thoughts of Zahrellion stole much of the enjoyment Jenka might have experienced watching her, but then Clover turned angry. Her look grew lustful and savage. When her hand clasped around Jenka's throat, her visage was one of sheer determination.

In the sitting lean Jenka had been frozen in, he had the most intimate of images flashing into his mind's eye. She wasn't choking him, for he needed no air. She was using his neck to steady herself while slowly grinding back and forth along his leg. She threw her head back, her scarlet locks shining in some sort of heavenly light, then she fell forward and put her head against his chest for a time.

After a while, Clover sat up quickly. "Sorry for this, but the pain will pass." She said the words as she pounded her fist into Jenka's chest so hard that it passed through his flesh and shattered his rib bones. Her grasp latched onto his very soul, and the yank that followed was so painful it stole Jenka's being. A flood of searing, blood-red agony engulfed him, and he screamed out for a very long time. He hoped for some sort of blackened unconsciousness to come save him, but none did.

He felt nothing but pain, hot and scarlet, and all consuming.

* * *

After entering the wyrm hole Golden had cast into existence, Aikira, March, and their wyrms came soaring out of the strange, swirling mist into a surreal scene that terrified them all, even the dragons.

The moon was high and the color of new cheese, but the sea was amber tinted, and the one land formation they could see was an upthrust of jagged black rock, which turned out to be a mound of some soft, gooey substance barely able to hold their weight.

Not a place of our worldsss, Blaze hissed into their heads. *Clover is farther away now.*

Your mental projection of our destination is what brought us here. Aikira defended her dragon's spell, if weakly. *We will cast another. This time concentrate on where you feel the old red.*

If this place wasn't so creeped out, I'd rather fly there, but right now I want to be anywhere but here. March pointed. *Look.*

In the distance the strange yellow sea was parted by a growing fin. Golden was going through the words of the spell and Blaze was trying to listen. March was thankful when the rippling circle appeared before them. They didn't hesitate to follow the Outlander through.

They went gliding down a long, perfectly cylindrical tunnel, watching land masses, oceans and starry skies twist and spin around them. It wasn't as bad as the first time, but the sensation was very disorienting. Plus, there was the unshakable feeling of dread for what could be waiting on the other side.

The tube closed tightly down on them, and March clenched his teeth and readied himself to battle whatever beast or army lay on the other side. But when they burst through the misty haze into reality, there was no threat.

Where are we now? Marcherion asked into the ethereal. They'd just come careening out of Golden's wyrm hole into a sky that was clean and fresh. A storm had just passed, and in the distance the dark wall of its rain could be seen creeping away. The rest of the immediate area was bathed in warm, rich afternoon sunlight. There was no land in sight, but there were birds, and Marcherion knew there was land somewhere nearby.

I don't know, Aikira said, with more than a little exasperation sounding in her tone. *Do you sense Crimzon?*

Blaze is trying.

March could feel what his dragon was sensing and was relieved. This time they were close. He and Blaze had both been practicing the words Golden spoke to open the wyrm hole. Had they known such a spell when they'd bonded, they could have avoided a year-long journey across vast oceans and formidable continents.

A moment later, March only shrugged when the young fire wyrm started banking them toward the darkness of the storm. *I guess he is this way.* March couldn't help but chuckle. *There is no other reason he would fly toward rain.*

Yesss, Blaze hissed to them. His displeasure rang clearly across the ethereal. *Into the ssstorm.*

Before long, all they could sense around them was whipping rain, gusting winds, and the hair-raising flashes of natural power that were streaking all about.

CHAPTER TWENTY

The pain lasted far longer than Jenka could have imagined. When it did end, Clover was there asking question after question about the Dragoneers. They were in some sort of plane constructed just for Xaffer's spell, or maybe by the demon bound to it. Time had little meaning, save for those agonizing moments. Jenka felt nauseous at best, and residual flashes of pain assailed him in brief, racking torrents. He felt as if every bit of skin had been ripped from his body, carefully and slowly. He managed to get the story of the Confliction out, but not much more. He also had the presence of mind to avoid telling Clover of Vax Noffa's part. The legendary wizard recluse had been her son, and the way he told the tale, Vax might have been long passed before the Dragoneers joined the fight.

Then it was Clover's turn to answer a question.

"How did you and Crimzon meet, or bond, or whatever?" asked Jenka.

"Well, that is a tale." Her form had less substance now that he was with her there. They were like shadows in an ill-lit room, but Jenka could make out the sheer adoration she had for her dragon in the excited way she gestured as she spoke about him.

"His mamra was wounded by hoard raiders. They stormed her lair, and Crimzon's hatchmate was killed, his mother given a mortal injury. Crimzon heard her songs, though, as she lay dying."

"Jade heard his mam's songs, too," Jenka interrupted. "They come to him sometimes as we are going along. Uh… they did." He missed his wyrm, not to mention Zahrellion and the child, but he held his sorrow in check and listened as Clover resumed her tale.

"Crimzon was forced to eat the flesh of the men his mam killed in the battle, all while watching her corpse rot." Her shadowy head fell into her hands and she sobbed. "I taught him to hunt for himself… I'll… I'll speak of something else." Her sniffle vanished as quickly as it appeared.

She reached over and placed her insubstantial hand on Jenka's forearm; he felt it there, but barely.

"There is a being who rules this space. He, it, will come to see the new arrival."

"Fyloch?" Jenka asked.

"No. This one calls itself Orthon, and it has been waiting for a dragon-blooded man to come so it can be released from this binding. It will be very displeased that you are not a dragon in human form."

"When will it come?"

"There is no way to convey time here, and no way to measure it. Your story might have taken decades to tell. When is irrelevant, but that he will come is certain."

Jenka wasn't looking forward to meeting this thing, but the vast knowledge he had gathered through the alien and the Dour hadn't vanished along with the magic. What he knew was his forever. His knowledge could never be taken. The alien had known much demon lore. Jenka couldn't help but ponder it.

He suddenly remembered that the druids of Dou had mind-washed men and ogres, and he decided that his mind could be lost. It was a disturbing thought.

He reached for the alien's knowledge and found it. The only problem was that thoughts of Zahrellion and their child kept creeping in. They reminded Jenka that he had failed in the most important parts of his life, and now he would never be there for them.

What if their child was twenty years grown now? What if it'd passed on and its children were grown? And what of Jade? The poor wyrm would die of sorrow, missing Jenka, if he hadn't already died in one of Xerrin Fyl's vile arenas. It was too sickening to bear, and Jenka began to crumble from the inside.

He and Clover absently continued speaking of things dragon riders would speak of. Her lust must have been quenched for she showed no more signs of desire, none at all. They found they were very similar, though. Both had left a lover and a child behind in order to keep their word. This led to Jenka crying out about his love for Zahrellion and the fear and worry he felt for a child he'd never known… would never know.

Both had also possessed large dragon tears cried by the mamra of their bond-mate. Jenka had retained both tears for a time and this amazed Clover, for just the one nearly stole her soul when she'd first grabbed it up.

Clover then told him how she had lost herself in the Dour at first. She and Crimzon had acted quite primal and dominated a continent for most of an age. That was before the alien crashed and the Sarax started cocooning. Once she realized that only if dragons and men fought together could they prevail against such a foe, she and the elves started preparing a future for the Dragoneers.

Jenka had no idea how much she had done, but when she started talking about Denner Noffa, he felt again how his child would miss him, and he his child.

Soon her voice carried away, and images of Zahrellion curled into a ball and sobbing filled his mind. A child screamed in terror, and then a cloudy roil of blood-colored steam rolled into their presence and Jenka felt a substantial amount of fear flow over him.

"Orthon," Clover said simply, and then their world was drenched in pain and blood.

* * *

Jade gasped a last bit of air before being taken back under. He saw Crimzon thrashing like a clutched fish in the octerror's grasp and felt hope. That hope was crushed just as Crimzon was bashed against the wall, then a glossy liquid film stole the scene from his eyes and he was dragged underwater.

He held his breath as long as he could, which for a dragon is a very long time; then just as the craving for fresh air was overpowering his will, he saw the creature's sharp, toothy beak coming closer. It opened and made to chomp down on him, but he let out his air and filled the thing's throat with noxious fuming spew. Even underwater, the stuff did potent damage, but Jade was left sucking in water instead of air, and the octerror, no matter how wounded by the green dragon's breath, hadn't loosened its grip on either of them. In fact, it began shaking Jade and slamming him against the submerged rocks, just as Jade imagined it was killing Crimzon above.

Jade tried one last time to wriggle free, but couldn't. The lack of air began pulling him out of consciousness, and water filled his cavernous lungs completely.

It was the end and Jade knew it.

There was nothing left that he could do.

CHAPTER TWENTY-ONE

Blaze and Golden fought the storm for a long while. They saw nothing, save for lightning, clouds and raindrops. It was as if there were no up or down, for the rain was flying sideways across their path. It was enough to make Marcherion angry. But then Blaze sensed Crimzon again and March grew excited. They were very close.

They lowered themselves into an even heavier part of the storm, and though it was harder to manage the sky, Blaze sighted the darkened hole where he sensed the old red.

Blaze dove toward the sea cavern as if he were flying on a string line. Golden and Aikira were right behind them. The storm was violent, and luckily the Outland girl was strapped into her saddle. Marcherion had ridden Blaze so much that they were a part of each other in flight, and even still he was having a time staying seated. Aikira's legs weren't nearly as strong, and the dragons had to twist and turn through the wet, turbulent air.

A brilliant flash of white-hot lightning crackled up uncomfortably close to them. For an instant, their hair stood on end and the air itself sizzled with static. The concussion of thunder that immediately followed sent both dragons careening off course and fumbling for purchase, but then they were below the clouds, skimming across a rocky shoreline toward a cave.

In a series of strobe flashes, they saw the huge bulk of an undulating green creature easing out into the sea. It was dragging not one, but two familiar forms through the shallows behind it.

Rock lions and lazy seals were floating everywhere, some dead, some half crushed or otherwise injured, some frolicking mindlessly. Hungry fish were swimming over each other in the shallows, gorging themselves on the carcasses. Whenever lightning flashed, the blackness of the waves was turned the bright color of blood. It was impossible to tell if the two dragons were alive, but Blaze and Golden were already corkscrewing around each other into a diving attack.

Sever the appendages holding them, Golden said into the ethereal. *Aikira and I will do the rest.*

Yes, we will, Aikira affirmed, and the two peeled off toward the bulbous creature's bulky end.

March lost them in the storm, while Blaze decided a direct approach was best and came down using claws and teeth to tear right through one of the thing's tentacles. The creature instinctually made to flee the surprise attack and started away. Crimzon's limp form didn't follow, but Jade's did. Aikira and Golden must have attacked just then, for the thing stopped moving into the sea and brought out three of its massive tentacles to defend itself.

Blaze had to dodge them with his wings while trying to get back into the dark sky, but he eventually managed to get clear of them. He went right for the tentacle that was wrapped around Jade and was slapped into the surf as a reward. He landed near where he had intended to attack, though. As Blaze rolled swiftly up out of the waves, March shook the steaming water from his hair and held his place steady with his thighs. At his breast his medallion began to burn with energy. The cherry conflagration filled his head and forced its way out. His eyes shone scarlet. Searing beams shot forth in a triangular pattern. Each of his eye rays charred whatever they touched, but the larger flow, from his wide-open mouth, burned deeply into the sea monster's flesh.

At the same moment, Aikira threw a pumpkin-sized ball of prismatic energy at the creature's body. The arcane mass wobbled through the air clumsily, but the impact was terribly volatile. Rubbery flesh and bright scarlet and white chunks of meat went flying everywhere. But even more effective at ridding them of this foe was the stark flash of bright illumination that scared the sea beast into forgetting its prey in order to flee.

At once, the great sea monster turned Jade loose and scurried into the sea. The battle was over, but the young green wyrm lay still.

Several hours and several dozen spells later, the four dragons and two riders lay in an exhausted heap inside the cavern. Blaze and Marcherion were standing guard because they'd done very little of the healing and were the most alert of the group.

It had been a close call with Jade. After only a few moments, Crimzon's brimstone core evaporated the water from his lungs and he began coughing and heaving and howling from the pain of his battered and broken bones. The water had to be spelled out of Jade, which hadn't been the problem. Getting the young wyrm to draw a breath after he was empty was the hard part.

The dragons tried several different spells, but nothing worked. Things grew tense as time passed. Though no one spoke it, they all knew there was a point where they would have to give up and leave the drowned dragon to his peace.

It was Aikira who finally talked Blaze through a method she'd seen work on a drowned sailor once. The larger fire wyrm nearly swallowed Jade's snout, but puffed him full of hot air as if he were a bellows. They did this only twice before Jade was hacking and thrashing around in a fevered state of confusion.

For Marcherion, it was an overwhelming relief. There he was thinking the green dragon was done one moment and having to duck to dodge Jade's tail the next. It was amazing, and March found a new, deeper sort of respect for Aikira. The girl's wyrm had gotten them here in just days, too. That fact wasn't lost on him. Crimzon and Jade both owed their lives to the Outlander and her wise wyrm.

After the elation of saving one of their own wore off, Aikira asked Jade about Jenka. The young dragon was exhausted and could manage very little. When they learned the bond connection between the two had been severed, everyone grew solemn again.

March was proud of his dragon for saving Jade, but he was worried for his friend. All Jade had been able to tell them was that Jenka had gone into a temple to the north. Looking out the cavern in the clear afternoon, March could see nothing in the northern distance but open sea. Nearer to the shore, the bloody sea-feast raged on. Fins of things huge and menacing slid through the water searching for a lagging rock lion, or a forgotten morsel of the last one savaged. This stirred a primal fear in his dragon. Just knowing there were things dragons were afraid of was enough to chill Marcherion's blood.

He hoped Aikira or Golden would wake soon, for he had every intention of flying north and scouting what was there. He would go first and look, then think of a plan while he rested. It was the smart, efficient thing for them to do.

CHAPTER TWENTY-TWO

The Coven Wisteria occupied a mansion on the harborfront southeast of Mainsted, but that wasn't the only place where the witches gathered. Ankha Vira's surprisingly sizable following had another residence, a respectable manor on the outskirts of southern Midwal. Herald said they couldn't get them all at once, but that didn't diminish Rikky's resolve in the least. Herald wasn't counting on Zahrellion to arrive at the Midwal coven, not with enough force to contain the witches there, but Rikky knew she wouldn't let them down. They'd traveled great distances and fought too many terrible battles together. He believed she would be there sooner than she needed to be.

Rikky hoped he could be at Midwal to meet her. If the surprise attack on the seaside mansion was swift and successful, he and Silva could hurry there and help.

"We will go in first and clear the way," Bhyront, a Grimwielder of higher rank, said. He, Herald, and Rikky were gathered in a field with two dozen other angry Grimwielders and Silva. Coming up a dirt track was another group of men that Herald had found willing to join them. The gathering wasn't very far from the Mainsted coven. Only a few days had passed since the incident in the market square, and there was a strong sense of urgency. "We owe them some payback and you some redemption."

"The gods must be a watchin' over me." Herald winked at Rikky. "I've had my fill of startled witches."

"You're not leading the men you rounded up on the second charge?" Bhyront asked.

"I am." Herald looked at his boots and shook his head. "I was once married to a witch. One time I snuck behind her while she was a brewing somethin'-or-another. I said boo, but the bug-eyed thing that turned and snapped at me made me shit my britches."

Rikky laughed and slapped Herald on the shoulder. "Mysterian did that to me once, too, only I didn't shit myself. I ran. Well, I hopped away as fast as I could."

"I just don't like surprising 'em, is all." Herald crossed his arms over his chest and beard in a manly fashion. "Killin' 'em is a whole different matter."

"I'll be right beside you, Herald." Linux stepped up out of nowhere, startling them all quite dramatically. "Please don't soil yourself this time."

"Why, I'll soil you, you fargin' druidoo," Herald snapped angrily. "Nearly shit myself again!"

"That rhymed, Herald," Rikky laughed and looked at the Grimwielder for support in his mirth. There was none there, and the man's serious demeanor reminded Rikky that they had some business to take care of.

"I'll need a signal for when the first men attack." Rikky took a breath and readied his mind for the battle. "If Silva and I come from the sea at the same time you enter, we can keep them spread out."

Bhyront begrudged him a nod of respect. Rikky smiled, but turned his attention to Linux's spiel.

"They'll have magic protection and alarming wards and such," the druid said, clearly using common terms so as not to confuse Herald. "I will need to go with the Grimwielders to counter the witches' craft, but I'll not go in with them. I'll wait for you, Herald, and the city men who've come."

I'll tell you exactly when they enter, Rikky, Linux continued in the ethereal.

Rikky could tell that Linux was sustaining some sort of casting that would keep their ethereal communications from reaching the witches. He hoped it wouldn't keep Zahrellion's voice from reaching them when the time came.

"If my Keepers got the word, they'll have a battalion riding for the Midwal place." Herald grew serious, too. "Let's get this witch hunt a goin'."

Rikky and his dragon were ready. After being helped up into his saddle, the young, one-legged Dragoneer got situated, then strung his bow. They took to the air and flew east for a time and then banked south before circling themselves high into the sky. They gathered an extreme amount of speed diving down into the knife-shaped, cliff-sided harbor. All the while they listened to Linux as he helped the Grimwielders through the witches' protective magic. When Linux announced the men's entry into the building, Silva started her gliding rise from the waves up toward the mansion.

Rikky guessed this place was probably where some illegal shipments made it into the city. It was far enough out from the heart of Mainsted to be beyond the Harbor Master's reach. It had winches at the top of the switchback, and below there was a wooden dock-house big enough to berth a sizable ship or two.

As he and his dragon came above ground level, a harpoon launched at them. The rope trailing it kept it from flying true, and it fell before it reached Silva.

An explosion of colorful witchy magic lit up the sky beyond the building. The air was filled with static. The smell of brimstone mixed with the brine, and then the dragon teardrop mounted in Rikky's bow filled him with a rush of Dour.

Battle-lust overcame him.

First, he used his bow to send a Dour-formed arrow at the harpoon gun that hadn't yet loosed. The shaft swiftly turned into a whirring flow of destructive energy. When it hit, mortar and stone caved in and crumbled into the interior in a completely unnatural manner.

Silva was already bathing the rear of the structure with her molten pewter spew. There were men there, loosing arrows and bolts up at them, but Rikky's Dour and Silva's protective magic shielded them from the missiles. Another whirring flow erupted from his bowstring and turned a balcony into rubble.

A witch found them from the garden, though. Her blistering fist of energy nearly thumped Silva out of the sky. Then three witches, two on brooms, and one apparently powerful enough to forego a flying device, came streaking out of an opening.

Amazingly, Silva tilted her head up and caught one of them with her spray. The witch, now covered in hardening metal, went down beyond the ledge and out of their vision like a falling chunk of stone.

The other broom rider rolled a ball of bright orange flames in her hands. She opened her palms before her face and blew. Her breath sent the inferno streaking across the space between her and Silva far too quickly. Rikky's dragon was forced to dive away and go below ground level.

Silva didn't waste energy. She curved around and started back up, swimming through the air in short, undulating bursts.

Rikky loosed another arrow the second he saw the broomless witch hovering over the garden. She let go of something, too. Rikky's shaft needled its way past the witch's magic and went straight through her heart. He saw this as her blast engulfed him in a choking concussion.

He saw the last broom-riding witch speeding away north and knew he had to shake off this sense of lethargy.

Then he realized he and his dragon were plummeting toward the bay.

CHAPTER TWENTY-THREE

Go, Rikky, go, Linux called. *They're not here. They must be in Midwal. We've taken the building. Zahrellion and the Keepers will need you.*

The word "Zahrellion" cut through the haze and found Rikky. He shook his head violently back and forth until he saw what was happening. He was spinning… Silva was spinning, but she was fighting it.

Rikky reached for the Dour he commanded and used it to give his dragon strength. Silva responded by forcing her wing where she wanted it to go. This happened just in time to avoid slamming into the sea. They didn't miss the wave-tops completely, and Rikky was splashed with surprisingly cool seawater. It served to knock the remaining cobwebs from his skull and blur his vision. By the time he was comfortable again they were streaking across the Frontier at an amazing clip.

Rikky was searching the sky for the broom rider, but didn't see her. He felt her, though, when her fiery spell impacted them. Having recently been similarly surprised by the ogres in the orchard, Silva avoided crashing into the trees. Instead, she curved her trajectory upward and snaked around in the sky to meet the witch.

The second fireball flew past them, its heat filling Rikky with resolve.

Rush her, Silva, Rikky commanded into the ethereal. *Charge right at her and peel off to the left.*

Yesss, the pewter-colored wyrm responded.

The witch was molding another orange ball of flame in her hands, but seeing the dragon coming right at her caused her to try to defend herself instead of attack. Rikky waited patiently as his dragon opened her maw to spray her breath. Silva let loose and curved left, while Rikky fired a Dour-formed arrow at a space yet unoccupied.

The witch, trying to avoid the dragon and its breath, moved her broom right into the arrow's path. In an explosion of magical force that blossomed outward but quickly sucked back in on itself, the witch was consumed. Nothing remained of her but part of a tumbling broomstick and a few bits of material lazily floating toward the ground.

Rikky wasted no more time fumbling around. As Silva carried them toward Midwal, he used his healing magic to make sure both he and his wyrm were able. After that, he cast forth some protective wards he'd learned from Jenka.

Way back when they were boys in Crag, Master Kember once said that the best way to deter the vermin was to make an example of the ones you had to kill. Rikky and Solmon saw a rotted goblin corpse hanging in the trees once. Standing there looking at it, he'd never thought that someday goblins would eat his leg and leave Solmon gutted by the lake. He reflected that his beloved Master Kember had been wrong for once. Those horrific displays had only angered the little beasties.

Even still, Rikky had every intention of making an example of the Coven Wisteria. All he had to do now was get there before they surprised Zah and Crystal with their numbers.

* * *

The being that was slowly unclenching the painful grip it had on Jenka and Clover was terrifying. A ghoulish set of cold blue eyes stared out from a meshed-metal-covered muzzle that wrapped around its mannish head. The mask formed into some semblance of a crown at the top and connected to the great chest piece the thing wore with lengths of silvery chain. Shoulder armor capped with molded sabre-cat skulls, and a jeweled belt bedecked the imposing form.

The demon was tall and lean. When his image was fully amongst them, the bone-spiked toe of a boot could be seen jutting out from under the priestly robes flowing under all the steel. The demon spun the forearm-thick shaft of a mace around once and slammed the butt end of it into the smooth surface on which he was standing. A thunderous boom echoed around them. When Orthon finally spoke, his voice cut into Jenka so deeply that he felt he'd rather die than endure it.

"What is this? Why is the binding not broken?"

When Jenka didn't respond, Orthon clenched his muscles in a rage and roared, "I asked you a question!"

Jenka didn't respond. He cowered there before the powerful being. He looked at Clover and saw that her projected image wasn't nearly as afraid. This gave Jenka some confidence and he instinctually reached for his dragon to draw some strength and resolve. Not finding Jade there was disheartening. He'd forgotten the link had been severed. Without his bond-mate, or the Dour sustaining him, he felt helpless. Still, he gathered his courage and stood before Orthon.

"Xaffer, the wizard who used you, is dead. You are bound here, but we are not. Release us from this place and restore us to our bodies and I swear I will find a way to end your binding."

"Bah!" The heavy end of the mace came over the demon's head and cracked down. Jenka had no substantial form. If he had, he would have been smashed flat. There was no flesh to damage, but the impact of the gigantic weapon hurt him nonetheless. He'd thought being ripped from the stillness was painful. This was a hundred times worse. He felt as if he'd actually been hammered flat, as if every bone were broken, and every cell destroyed. He thought diving into a vat of molten forge-metal might soothe such a feeling as this. Luckily, the pain eventually carried him away.

He dreamed of Zahrellion and his unborn child, but it was no hazy day-vision like he often had when he was on his dragon's back. Lemmy was looming over a crib with a knife held partially concealed in his fist. Zahrellion was in full battle gear but staring aimlessly out the window of the tower in which they were all standing. Jenka strode over to her, but when she turned it was Orthon's iron-masked gaze that met him.

The demon's eyes flared with laughter. He reached up and tore off his crown mask and Zahrellion's beautiful face was there, but only for an instant. Then it was Orthon's ugly, mutated visage.

The demon had sharp, jagged teeth with thin lips that didn't close all the way over them when he swallowed. His long, pink tongue was forked, and he licked his upper teeth every few seconds. His nose was skullish, just two open holes. The demon's eyes, though, were as blue as the sky.

Orthon wasn't as intimidating when he was the same relative size as Jenka. But Jenka still felt the pain of the mace blow. He wouldn't dare provoke another crushing.

"Why should I believe you?" the demon asked before restoring his crowned mask to his head.

Jenka wasn't expecting the question, and it took him a moment to force out the feelings of longing he'd just been consumed with. He wasn't certain how he should respond, but the words came to him, as did the reasoning behind them. These thoughts flowed to him in the memory of a dragon song sung by Jade's mam. She'd sung it just before she cried the teardrop that was mounted in his sword back in the world where his body existed. "Because you have nothing to lose by trusting me, and this may be the only chance in all of time you ever get to be released from a dead wizard's spell."

"I know these things," Orthon growled and snatched Jenka by the collar of his triangular chest armor. "Why should I trust any measly mortal?"

Again the words just came. "Because I once swore to do everything I could to save Clover from this fate. That promise brought me all the way here before you. How could you not trust any being who would willingly go this far?"

"Why hasn't the bond already been broken?" Orthon asked. The demon was clearly considering Jenka's suggestion, but now he was waiting for an answer.

"Because I am not of dragon blood." Before Jenka could finish responding, the demon roared and the mace pummeled him flat again. This time, when the pain carried him away, it was to a place far less pleasant.

CHAPTER TWENTY-FOUR

Zahrellion knew immediately that she'd swooped into a nest of expectant hornets. Crystal failed to freeze any of the witches she blasted. They were somehow protected from the dragon's frigid spew. The sky filled, far too quickly, with more mind-stretched women riding poorly enchanted broomsticks, and it soon looked as if a beehive full of filthy tavern girls had been kicked over.

Crystal's angry magic did some damage—far more than the witches must have anticipated. Most of them couldn't even be considered witches, Zahrellion decided. They were mostly just girls taught to blow a ball of fire and ride a stick. When Zahrellion started casting powerful druidic spells and a hundred Keepers rode into the mix, the odds looked to even out a little bit, but only long enough for them to catch their breath.

Crystal was nearly as old as Golden, and she was a vastly capable wyrm. She kept the witches' fiery kisses from reaching her and her rider. She also shielded some of the Keepers who had ridden a very long time to meet them there. The big, white-scaled frost dragon even bashed one witch into oblivion with her tail, but her breath was useless, and a streak of lightning eventually came up and bit her.

Scales were sizzled, and some of the meat beneath them was crisped from the heat of the strike, but Crystal kept them in a position to protect the Keepers. This allowed Zahrellion to take in the scene. It didn't take long to find the source of her dragon's current pain.

In the yard before the manor was a trio of witches all hovering in an outward-facing triangular formation. Their dark hair was blowing wildly in several different directions. In the middle of the three, and hovering slightly higher, was Ankha Vira. She was building up another mass of crackling yellow energy to shock Crystal with. A handful more of the hovering witches were scattered in a rough circle around their leader, but they were attacking more than guarding.

Arrows were flying in arcing volleys between the Keepers and the hired mercenaries battling alongside the coven's fervent followers. A few dozen men lay dead already, and more were falling every minute. Over there an arrow-riddled witch lay dying. Over here a knot of young men fought furiously against a pair of seasoned Keepers. They were probably just stupid boys in love with the half-crafty harlots swarming the sky. They must have been in love, for even as the Keepers slaughtered them, more came charging in.

Zahrellion held fast as Crystal darted out of the way of Ankha Vira's next blast of lightning. It was a near thing, but having avoided it, Zah found she was just glad these were not Sarax in the sky. This many Sarax could savage a dragon in a few heartbeats.

An illusion built on a few spells, and a false sense of confidence, was all these foes really were. Ankha Vira and her three protectors might be a little more formidable, but Zahrellion doubted it.

Ravage them, Crystal. Tear them from the sky, Zah ordered before focusing her druidic magic on the coven's leader.

Crystal went slithering through the air around the broom-riding novices. Her tail and her snapping jaws found flesh over and over again. Several of the men fighting below were crushed by falling witches, and for a time blood rained down on them.

The battle on the ground took a dramatic turn then. Just before Zahrellion sent a powerful fist of energy at Ankha Vira, the leader of the coven cast a summoning.

From a hole that had opened up below the witch, small goblin-sized demons and a few multi-legged devils came scurrying forth.

Like being hit in the chest with a ship's timber swung by a giant, Ankha Vira was battered away from her protective triad by the impact of Zahrellion's spell. Crystal blasted the hole with her breath and the creatures froze solid. Dozens of them escaped, though, and they quickly began killing Keepers and coven followers alike.

The men were terrified of them. Even the seasoned Keepers were having a time holding their ground.

The hovering witches all cast a simultaneous spell that took the frost dragon by surprise. Great launching pulses of magic formed into ropes that wrapped around Crystal, and only Zahrellion's quick thinking gave them a chance.

Land and twist around as swiftly as you can, Zah said as she hunkered into her saddle and held on as best she could. When Crystal's claws touched ground, the dragon used them to launch her body into a twisting spin.

The witches strung to her by their spells were whipped so suddenly that they came around Crystal's body and slapped hard against her icy scales. One of them went limp because her head was jerked back so hard her neck snapped. Her magic rope fell away and she thumped awkwardly into the turf. Others were trampled under the dragon, and when Crystal let out a battle roar, two of the remaining witches fled for their lives.

Ankha Vira and her guards were still there, though, as was another person Zah would have never suspected seeing.

Lemmy?

What the leader of the Coven Wisteria was holding in her clutches now did nothing less than stop Zahrellion cold.

"You are powerless now, Dragoneer!" the witch yelled. "Call off your attack!"

Zahrellion hated to do it, but she had no choice. Ankha Vira was holding Jericho in her arms. The witch was softly cooing at him while staring victoriously back at Zah.

"If you hurt him I will spend all my days tormenting you," Zahrellion said through clenched teeth. She started to blast Lemmy with a verbal tirade but saw that he was changing into the form of a witch now. It hadn't been Lemmy at all, and she suddenly knew that Rikky and his attack on the Mainsted coven hadn't been the surprise they had hoped for either. The witch posing as Lemmy had heard all of their plans.

"Call them off." Ankha Vira shook baby Jericho, causing Zahrellion's heart to flutter up into her throat.

"Stop," Zahrellion said simply, and the few battles still raging around them slowed to a still. The death scream of a man battling one of the demons must have reminded Ankha Vira that she needed to restrain her fighters, too. With a wave of her hand, her unworldly little band of creatures stood down as well.

One of the witches wrapped the baby's ankle with a braided bracelet and then took her from the High Witch.

Zahrellion knew the anklet was no ornamental offering, but something like a collar.

Ankha Vira wore her triumph with a satisfied grin. "We will raise him to be a just king, I assure—"

Just then a streaking arrow formed of Dour came straight down out of the sky, nearly impaling the witch who was holding the baby. Half a heartbeat later, two roars resounded, one from a silvery-colored dragon, one from a one-legged boy.

They were the sweetest sounds Zahrellion had ever heard.

CHAPTER TWENTY-FIVE

Rikky wasn't sure if his arrow had sliced through the binding twine or not, but he felt his aim had been spot on. Baby Jericho wasn't screaming in pain, and the witch holding him was crumpling from her wounds. Then Silva was leveling out of her dive into a terribly tight corkscrew, trying to slow them. She vomited her molten spew across one of the hovering Wisterites, and the witch fell from the sky, screaming as she went. The sound ended with her impact and served as a warning for the rest of the coven.

Ankha Vira had Jericho again. All of her remaining followers, and her hellborn devils, were drawing in around her to protect her. The leader of the Coven Wisteria was trying to teleport herself away, and Rikky couldn't let that happen. He had no idea how to stop it, though, so he took a chance and asked Silva to dive for the baby.

Rikky saw that Zahrellion was getting herself together. Crystal was icing over the coven's followers on the ground. This allowed the few dozen remaining Keepers to storm the gathering knot of witches.

Practiced blade met witchy spell, and bloody magic filled the air again.

Ankha Vira was near to completing her next spell when Silva's claws reached out for her. There was no way to snatch the baby by himself without crushing him. Even grabbing them both was risking injury to the child, but it had to be done. There was the loud crackling sound of a spell releasing and then a whirring of impossibly radiant color. Rikky could tell Silva had latched onto the witch and Zah's baby, but something else happened as well.

The world around them flashed away, and they were suddenly in a meadow just a few hundred yards from where they'd been.

Silva roared out to let Crystal know their location as the witch blasted outward, causing her to release her claws. They'd been teleported with the witch, but not very far.

It was almost comical how the twenty or so remaining fighters from each side of the battle came running over toward where they appeared. Only a handful of witches could be seen at all. And here came Crystal, too. Zahrellion had a look of terror on her usually determined face. She pointed as her dragon carried her past Silva's hover.

Rikky craned his head around to see what had her looking so stricken. Ankha Vira still had Jericho, and the witch was casting another teleportation spell. There was no way Silva or Crystal could get there this time, and even if Silva could, her damaged claws couldn't grab them again. Rikky wasn't even sure how his dragon would land, but he would heal her once she did.

As Zahrellion closed on the witch and her son, the two vanished away with a sizzling pop. Even more surprising was that the rest of the coven and the unearthly creatures all disappeared, too.

Circle up high, Silva, Rikky said. *Maybe we can see where they appear.*

There, Silva hissed and was streaking away toward a cloud of dust blooming from a small road. Rikky readied his bow, but it turned out to be just two untethered horses instinctually fleeing the arcane chaos of the battle.

Rikky had Silva circle up even higher. His dragon complied, but he could feel her pain. After a few more minutes of seeing nothing from the higher vantage, they flew back near the regrouping Keepers and found a soft place for Silva to get her ruined claws down.

Immediately, Rikky started healing her.

Not long after, Zahrellion walked over and joined them. It was dark, and Rikky had started a real fire.

"Where is Crystal?" Rikky asked.

"Making a wider sweep of the area." Zah's dark, saddened eyes never looked up. "I want to thank you."

"For losing Jericho to a stupid witch?" Rikky wasn't pleased about anything, other than the way Silva's wounds had closed for him.

"That was brave, what you did." Zahrellion fought back more tears. Rikky didn't even bother to hide his. "Just getting here from Mainsted is a feat to be heralded. And you almost got him back," she finished.

Rikky's face twisted in the moonlight. "Jenka would have managed it," he bawled. Zahrellion came closer to comfort him.

"We have prisoners to interrogate," Zahrellion told him through a sniffle, while stroking his hair with a half-sisterly, half-motherly sort of affection.

"They left some of the more injured novices behind. We will soon know where they took him. It will take them some time to enchant another binding anklet."

"I got it?" Rikky asked hopefully.

Told yousss, Silva hissed, causing her rider to chuckle, despite his gloom.

"You did," Zah nodded. "It wasn't on him when they flashed away."

"Are they like ogre collars?" Rikky shrugged away any bits of pride he felt for slicing the anklet with his shaft. "I just knew it was a bad thing when I saw it."

"I hope not." Zahrellion heaved a sigh of her own, only her sigh was one of resolve. "Now, let's go see if we can find out where they've taken him. I want him back, Rikky. I want my son back."

CHAPTER TWENTY-SIX

Jenka came around when the butt of Orthon's mace-shaft thumped into the floor again. With the sound came a rushing relief from the pain.

"I will release only one of you," Orthon told him. "The other, I will hold until the binding comes loose. You must choose."

For a long time Jenka contemplated his situation and the implications of everything. Something was there that he couldn't quite see yet. Nevertheless he didn't try to grasp at it. Instead, he thought about the worst of his feelings: how he'd grown up fatherless, how his friends Grondy and Solmon, and beloved Master Kember had met their deaths so early; how his dragon was without a bond-mate, and how his friends were unable to depend on him. He was a terrible father, a terrible friend, and an even more terrible mate to Zah. He wasn't strong like Clover. He was just a fumbling boy fighting in a man's boots. He had done little but hurt those who loved him. They were better off, would remain better off, without him.

Those were the thoughts running through Jenka's head when he decided, but none of them was the reason he chose the way he did. Despite thinking about all of those negative things, one ray of hope shone through. It was a tiny morsel to cling to, but it was a hope he latched onto anyway.

"Clover?" Jenka asked the darkness around them. He wasn't certain if she was even in their vicinity. "You're the more powerful," Jenka said. "I'll send you back."

"How will I undo the binding?" she asked, forming up out of the darkness. "I think it should be you. You deserve to leave this place. I have done things worthy of such a prison."

"Your dragon needs you," Jenka said. "Trust me in this. You can make the grandson undo Xaffer's spell. Xerrin Fyl will be putty in your hands."

"I'm sure I can, but why would you risk yourself for me?"

"Because I kept my word to your dragon, and I know the two of you won't forget that." Jenka wanted to tell her there was more to his reasoning, but couldn't without Orthon hearing him. "All you have to do is make Xerrin Fyl undo his grandfather's spell."

"I won't leave you here with him," Clover huffed. "How could I?"

"You have no choice." Orthon batted Clover away. "I know you do not crave the pain, as you say, wench."

"Send her back to her own form, on her own plane," Jenka said through his fear.

"I won't forget you," Clover whispered as she started to be torn out of that moment and thrust into another.

"It doesn't matter." Jenka hurried his words. "If Xerrin Fyl does not undo his grandfather's binding, then you have to kill him for sending me here. Even if he does undo it, you have to kill him, Clover."

"I understand now." Her words barely reached Jenka, but knowing she understood filled him with some relief. He hoped he was right about Xerrin Fyl's spell. If he wasn't, he had just traded places with Clover forever.

* * *

Blaze dove first, but Crimzon, flying on wings now fixed with Outlander wizardry, sped past the smaller fire wyrm toward the temple below. Jade still outflew them both and got there before the others. He barely had time to cast a pulse of magic into being and hurl it at the newer temple's bell tower when a wide-spreading, lavender-colored ray shone up and caught him in its beam. He didn't feel the effects of Xerrin Fyl's spell at first, but then he found he couldn't leave the light in which he was trapped. Worse, Blaze came storming in and spraying dragon fire everywhere, only to get trapped in the sky right there over the structure with him.

Below them, dozens of priests and acolytes came out and began casting pulsing magic missiles and more powerful fists of energy up at the two trapped dragons.

It was clear none of them had been expecting two dragons, so when Crimzon avoided the wizard's trap and blasted half of them to ash, it was a total surprise. Then Golden entered the fray. Her molten spew was deadly, but Aikira was so weary from recasting the complex spells needed to repair Crimzon's wings that she was of little help.

Marcherion, trapped beside Jade in the funnel-shaped lavender beam radiating up from the temple, was trying to let his anger force the Dour out of him, but it wouldn't come. Jade couldn't use magic either. The two of them could barely fly. When March's frustration reached its limits, and his dragon was tired of dodging pesky, stinging spells from the priests below, they decided to land right on the source of the radiant energy.

Blaze's bulk shadowed the light from Jade long enough for the young green wyrm to escape the air over the temple, but Blaze couldn't get his claws on the ground, as he had hoped. He ended up stuck in the ray, just that much closer to the priests in the yard.

Another man came storming out then; this one was wearing a high-collared robe of deep blue. His attack did far more than sting, and by the time his display of brilliant flashing, multi-colored power had exhausted itself, Marcherion was limp and barely clinging to his dragon, while Blaze had to fight with all his strength just to stay aloft.

Golden saw the source of the trapping spell and used her own Dour to cast a powerful counter.

It took a moment to take effect, but then all at once the ray of light vanished as the earth around the enchantment's source stone exploded into a crater large enough to bury a supply wagon.

The Soulstone? Crimzon wondered, tasting the familiarity of the item on his forked tongue. He immediately went back into the fray to take a look. He had to dive down into the temple yard to see it, and while he was there he set a good portion of the structure aflame.

More priests came storming out. Great red streaks of magic shot up at the wyrms circling over them, but their feeble craft did little damage. It was only the power of the Soulstone that had been sustaining the trap.

Crimzon made to land in the crater Golden's magic had caused, but a few of the priests, these with a glowing aura of protection surrounding them, were already digging through the carnage looking for the prized artifact.

Blaze and Marcherion floundered in the temple yard, but only until Crimzon wormed his way into it with them. The huge old red forced them to lift up and start circling as he used his foreclaws like a dog digging for a bone, and started sifting through the debris looking for the magic he sensed.

"You'll not have my grandfather's prize, wyrm!" Xerrin Fyl said as he stepped out of a set of huge, banded double doors on a third-level balcony and blasted a chunk out of Crimzon's arse. Crimzon whacked him, balcony and all, to the ground with his tail before leaping awkwardly into flight. Just for good measure, the old fire dragon set even more of the newer temple on fire as he went. The pain from his gushing wound, however, kept him from going far.

CHAPTER TWENTY-SEVEN

"It's here!" one of the priests called. "I've found it."

Xerrin Fyl appeared next to the man. He was covered in blood from a gash in the forehead, and three of his fingers were bent askew from his balcony tumble, but he had no problem snatching the Soulstone from the man and flashing away again.

Golden's molten spew splashed across the area only half a beat after the wizard was gone. The priests there, who had been digging, were coated. They crumpled into sizzling fetal balls as the golden stuff cooled and hardened over their skin.

Xerrin Fyl started casting spells on some of his own priests then. The Soulstone turned them into huge, raging demon-fighters. Crimzon watched from where he was tending his wound as Blaze swept by and blasted one of the three giant man-things with his breath, but another of them grabbed and yanked down on Blaze's hind leg and he and Marcherion crashed into a block-and-mortar wall.

For a long moment it looked as if the whole temple would collapse, but it didn't. Instead, Blaze went limp inside the bailey, and the giant priest they had just scorched began pounding the red wyrm with its barrel-keg-sized fists, while another grabbed hold of a wing and tried to twist it off.

Crimzon blasted his own arse with dragon fire and roared. The pain wasn't so bad, and the wound all but stopped bleeding. Strangely, the old dragon was suddenly invigorated. He was feeling something he hadn't felt in a very long time.

Clover!

Could it be?

He *could* feel her, and he leapt into the sky so that he could better seek out the source of the feeling. There was no surprise when he found it was coming from deep below the two burning temples. The surprise came when he was suddenly filled with a powerful rush of Dour through their bond-link.

* * *

Jade wanted to land and get Marcherion out of the bailey area. Blaze's rider was lying still, and above them a few men were starting to loose arrows down from a window. Luckily, they were not skilled with the bow, for had they been, March would have been shafted a dozen times by now.

Jade, not sure what he should do, swooped down and braved the yard. One shaft bounced off of his scales, while another stuck firmly in his neck. It hurt considerably but was by no means a mortal wound. One of the giants turned, but it was too far away to get at them. Marcherion was in Jade's grasp when he lifted back up; that was all that really mattered. He carried the limp Dragoneer out of the fray while Golden dove in to help their red-scaled friend.

Jade left Marcherion lying on one of the elevated seaside ledges he'd used while waiting for Jenka, then returned to the battle. There was no way they were going to leave Blaze unprotected. It was no surprise when Jade found Golden and her rider settling in over the fallen wyrm to defend him.

Aikira cast a spell that knocked the enlarged priest away from Blaze's wing, but the one bashing at his head and neck was still there. Arrows rained down, and one actually grazed Aikira's face. Jade sensed her anger from across the sky and made to help her attack. She turned to blast at the archers, but Jade was already there, claws gripped to the very mortar like a great garden-wall lizard as he filled the room with his poisonous breath through the window.

He was glad beyond measure that she restrained from casting the spell on her lips. Then one of the men dove out of the opening rather than choke on the terrible green fog. His scream reminded Jade to watch out. The backswing of the hammering giant nearly hit him as he passed. It caught the man who'd jumped, and his scream ended abruptly as he went spinning away.

Golden knocked the huge, pounding thing back and landed over Blaze's still body so that the giant couldn't keep striking the red dragon. Jade dropped down and joined her, and with their tails bumping behind them, they fought back to back to protect their companion.

Xerrin Fyl used the Soulstone to cast again. Two more of his followers, this time two of the blue-robed men, began to transform. Where the other beasts had transformed into huge things bent on blunt brutality, these giant bipeds were built to move swiftly. The arms of the two men elongated, and their hands transformed into thin, dagger-long claws. Their legs fattened, and muscles bulged under prickly pink skin. Their faces pushed out into wolfish snouts, and their eyes were skinned over. In their place, a pair of finger-thick stalks wavered forth. At the ends of them were different eyes. These eyes were the size of melons and looked to be made of swirling green flame. They took in the two defending dragons, and both of them stormed past the other giants and began zapping Golden and Jade with short, terrible jolts of searing static.

The dragons used their teeth and claws, as well as spells both defensive and offensive. With his breath, Jade saturated the stalk-eyed giant attacking him. The thing was choking in a cloud of it, but only for a few moments. It gathered itself and then zapped the young green wyrm so badly he fell, jaw first, into an up-swinging clawed foot.

* * *

Aikira looked around and realized she and Golden were the last ones left to defend Blaze. Luckily he was stirring, because she didn't think she could handle all of these giant freaks for long. When the next creepy bug-eyed thing came at them, it was deftly bathed in a gout of molten dragon breath. It was still floundering on the ground, but there was another, and two of the other giants who hadn't yet taken injury.

Blaze shifted and tried to roll to his feet, but the third giant brute, the one he had scorched, came around and started kicking him. Aikira couldn't pay much attention to them now, though. The rest of the freakish giants were trying to circle around her dragon before it could lift away.

Aikira hated to do it, but she felt it was their best chance. Her heart told her to stand over Blaze and protect him, but her mind said otherwise.

She had her dragon leap for the air, knowing they could do more damage with sweeping passes than stumbling around. Golden's wings snapped open and they were up, but then came the long-legged, bug-eyed giant, leaping for them like some gargantuan frog.

Golden had to draw in her tail, and still it missed them by just a hair's breadth.

Aikira's dragon shifted in the sky, moving herself above the reach of the giants, but a ball of unholy fire exploded over them. Fearing for her rider's condition, Golden bolted through the air like a scalded dog until they were a good distance away from the battle.

Aikira was blistered across the shoulder, neck, and face, and her hair was mostly gone. The smell of it made her want to retch. She thought maybe her right biceps and forearm were cooked, but she somehow mastered the pain.

When she urged her dragon back into the fray, they found Blaze had new protectors.

It was Crimzon and Clover. And the fire-haired warrior who'd built a magic castle in anticipation of the Dragoneers and sacrificed motherhood so the world might be rid of the terrible alien was everything Aikira could have hoped to behold.

The legendary warrior and her fire wyrm tore into Xerrin Fyl's handful of giants as if they were nothing more than a pack of schoolyard bullies.

PART IV
TOGETHER AGAIN

CHAPTER TWENTY-EIGHT

Clover was a bit surprised that it was an ebon-skinned girl riding the golden dragon speeding into the battle. It wasn't so much because the rider had darker-pigmented skin, it was that the girl's skin went so perfectly with the honey amber sparkle of her wyrm's scales that they had to have been created for each other. The girl looked like some goddess of old. They fought well enough, that was certain.

The Dragoneer and her wyrm were capable, it was clear, but Clover had found her dragon tear lying beside Jenka's petrified form, mixed in with his things. The Dour gave her strength and stamina, while the golden dragon grew weary.

Oh, how Clover had longed to feel that power again, and it had come back to her so easily only because of that determined boy.

She was soon fighting in a focused rage. The rush was intense, and she felt redeemed and free.

The dragon tear's power kept them moving faster and sharper than Xerrin Fyl and his quickly diminishing forces, but there was something else.

Clover was aging at a quickened rate. The years she'd been spelled were catching up to her physical body, and it was terrifying. So much so that she was having a hard time concentrating on the battle now.

There is the Leif Repline Fountain in the Giant Mountainsss, Crimzon told her. *It has the power to restore usss. We will kill this wizard for Jenka, then go there to live or die together.*

"I'm lucky I found you." Clover actually laughed. Even after a few decades of separation, her dragon knew how to turn her mood and give her substantial hope with just a few spoken words. They were dropping down amid the giants again now, each eager to get this done so they could seek the legendary fountain of replenishment. If it really existed, it could heal them both completely.

Crimzon's claw ripped across the chest of one of the giant brutes, while Clover swung her fist over her head and smacked it into her open palm before her, causing a ripple of energy to explode forth.

Crimzon roasted the gashed giant where he stood and then braced his claws on the ground. The back flow from Clover's devastating ripple spell was nearly as destructive as the rest of the casting.

Before them, two giants were swept off of their feet and thrown through the toppling walls of the smoldering temple structure. It was all coming down now, and the few enemies left were trying to flee. The remaining stalk-eyed giant was trying to get hold of Golden. Clover just wanted to find Xerrin Fyl and kill him. Her bones were starting to creak, and her hair was graying before her eyes.

Can you sense the Soulstone? she asked her dragon.

Only when he isss usingss it.

Where did you sense it last?

From the entryss of the old templesss.

He is seeking another of his grandfather's artifacts, I'd wager. Clover's laugh held far less mirth than it had only a short while earlier. *My skin is spotting, Crim. I feel like I'm a hundred years old.*

You aress more than a hundred yearsss old, Cloverss. And look, we've found our wizard.

* * *

Aikira dispatched one of the giants, and while gathering her breath, watched Crimzon and Clover battle three of the creatures, ending one in flames, and then two more with a blast that leveled the whole structure of the newer palace. All of this while looking off in a half-dreaming daze.

Aikira was as envious as she was awe struck by the grace with which Clover gestured her spells from dragonback. And Crimzon had never looked so fierce. When they banked up and over near the older temple building, Aikira urged Golden to take them there, too. Then suddenly Crimzon was back-flapping awkwardly over them as he tried to get clear of something.

Apparently, Xerrin Fyl had spelled himself with the Soulstone this time, for he was busting through the smoldering rooftop of his grandfather's temple with a sword in his hands that was growing with him. The blade sounded as if it were humming and had a glowing amber cast to its sheen. Xerrin Fyl's facial features never changed, save for his eyes sinking in a bit, and the wildness of his hair, but he was reaching a staggering size. When he raised his sword, he was as big as the old dragon.

Golden was suddenly forced to dive under a whooshing pass of the glowing blade. It was enormous, too, and all of the sky over both temples was within its reach.

When he came spinning around a second time, Aikira and her dragon were caught with the flat of the blade and slapped hard to the ground. It was a good thing, too, for Crimzon and Clover sped right over the swinging weapon, and Clover used the power of her dragon tear to cast another slice of energy.

This time, the devastating ripple tore through Xerrin Fyl's giant throat like some invisible razor. The attack left him stumbling backward while trying to keep his life's blood from spraying out of him.

Aikira, astride Golden, saw that the enemy was demoralized by this. Many began to flee. She immediately went to see how badly the other dragons were injured. She had no idea where Marcherion was, and she was worried sick for him. It was no surprise when Crimzon landed near them and started looking over Blaze's wounds, but when Aikira saw Clover, she was shocked into open-mouthed silence.

"Yes, I'm an old maid," Clover said. Her teeth had fallen out and her face was that of an ancient woman. She was so terribly dressed for her figure that Aikira felt shame for her.

"Tell Jenka we kept our word and killed Xerrin Fyl," the feeble old woman on Crimzon's back said.

"If we're lucky, we won't die getting where we have to go."

"Are you all right?" Aikira asked stupidly. Then an idea struck her. "I know how to use the wyrm holes. If you know where in the world you want to go, I can send you there."

Immediately, Crimzon began questioning Golden about the wyrm holes and how to use them. Clover seemed like she might have died already. She was sitting as still as a statue when Jade carried Marcherion back down to the battlefield.

The oldest Dragoneer was angry about being left on a sea cliff, but his arm was broken, and half of his head looked like a pumpkin. Jade almost dropped him as they came down.

"I feel Jenkass againsss," Jade hissed happily. "He is coming."

"Killing that foul wizard is what broke the spell holding him." Clover's voice was nearly a whisper. The last was barely said at all. "Orthon won't be happy."

CHAPTER TWENTY-NINE

When Jenka poked his scruffy brown-haired head out of the shattered door of the old temple, Aikira couldn't wait to tell him about his child and all the things that had been going on back home. It was growing dark, and flies and carrion birds were easing in closer to the carnage to get a taste. But when she saw the look on his face, and the way he was fumbling his sword belt around his waist as he hurried toward his dragon, she could tell he was terrified of something. Then he saw Clover, all old and frail, and he fell to his knees.

"I'm so sorry, Clover." He held his head and was clearly fighting tears. For some reason this caused Aikira to envy Zahrellion just a little bit.

"Don't be sorry." Clover smiled a wrinkled old smile. "I'm not dead yet."

Blaze had turned his neck and head around and was watching from beside his rider. Marcherion's eyes were pooled with thick tears. Aikira knew they both looked up to Crimzon as the alpha fire drake. It was clear the old red was about to leave them.

She would miss him, too.

Meeting Crimzon in that dwarven flue was one of the most terrifying moments of her life, and she would never forget him. Her tears had been flowing since she'd seen Jenka alive, but now she was bawling.

"Orthon is coming," Clover said to Jenka. Now her whitened hair was falling loose. "It will not count against your honor if you leave him be."

Goodbye Dragoneersss, Crimzon hissed, and with that he rubbed his eyelids against his foreclaw and then leapt into the sky.

The Dragoneers and their dragons watched as the pair grew smaller and then disappeared altogether into the wyrm hole Crimzon called forth.

* * *

Jenka had to duck and dodge his dragon's sloppy-tongued greeting. He was pleased to see Jade again, but they didn't have time to enjoy each other. Orthon really was coming, and he was as angry as any being had ever been. He was still bound to the trap, but Jenka wasn't sure how far the demon could roam from it. The fact that he was now starting to manifest himself in their plane was a shocking development. Jenka had tricked him, and now held the demon's eternal fate in his hands.

Orthon had been bound to the trap by Xaffer's spell, as was Clover. Only Orthon or Xaffer could have released her. Xerrin Fyl had sent Jenka there, not his grandfather, and when Clover killed the younger mage, the spell he hastily cast on Jenka died with him. Orthon had no part in imprisoning the Dragoneer and he couldn't have stopped Jenka's release had he tried. He was left with no one to guarantee his unbinding and Jenka expected to swiftly learn what limitations the demon did or didn't have.

After feeling a taste of the pain Orthon had to offer, Jenka really wanted no further part of him; at least that is the way he felt until he grabbed his sword by the hilt and checked the draw.

The instant the blade started out of the scabbard, the Dour from the teardrop mounted in the hilt filled him. This must have ignited the Dour that had saturated him when he was inside the alien because the sea of magic stuff that engulfed him was vast and deep.

Fear was no longer a part of it.

Where is Rikky? Jenka asked through the ethereal.

Probably trying to kill the witches who tried to take Jericho, March responded.

Jericho?

Jenka, Aikira's voice entered the conversation through a sniffle. *You have a son. Zahrellion named him Jericho after your father.*

But Jericho wasn't my father. Jenka was suddenly regretful for thinking such a thing. In his heart, Jericho De Swasso had been his father. He stopped thinking and began dreaming about a boy he'd never seen, a giggling infant with eyes the color of submerged coral, like his, all bundled in silky cloth.

Jenka was starting to flow away into a Dour dream until Orthon spoke with his terrible, booming voice. The demon had finished manifesting himself amid the rubble, but Jenka had little concern for it now.

"There are more of you?" the mesh-masked demon roared as he looked around at the bloody battlefield. "How dare you trick me, boy? I am going to—"

"You are going to sit still, you moronic hell-born giboon! You are barely even here." Jenka yelled from Jade's back. He wasn't sure what a giboon was, but he'd heard March call Rikky one at least a hundred times. He was glad that Orthon wasn't able to peel himself further from Xaffer's bind. As it was, the demon could probably only manage a spell or two from where it was. "If you kill me, Orthon, I won't be able to break your bind."

The demon was now twice as large as the giants lying there, but not nearly as big as the dead wizard's corpse. Jenka turned to look down at Marcherion, who was just getting mounted on Blaze's back. *What is this of witches and my child? Why are you not there protecting them?*

I came to help you and Crimzon.

Jenka weighed this and the way Marcherion's head looked like a misshapen lump.

It's just some uprising that started in the unruled mainland, Aikira said. *Rikky and Queen Zahrellion will have taken care of it by now.*

Queen Zahrellion? Unruled mainland? How long was I trapped with Clover?

"Not long enough," Orthon grumbled loudly. "Break the bind, boy, as you swore to do."

"Xaffer had to use the Soulstone to bind you," Jenka snapped at the demon. "He wasn't powerful enough to do it himself. The stone is your binder." Jenka pointed at the enlarged corpse of Xerrin Fyl. The knowledge had just flowed into him and he understood the way of things. The Dour had him feeling invincible, too, and he spoke with disdain to the powerful thing that had once tortured him and Clover. "It is there. Destroy it yourself. That mace should do just fine."

Under his mask, Orthon licked his exposed upper teeth with a loud slurp and grunted. His glowing blue orbs narrowed tightly, and he hissed. Then he went directly to Xerrin Fyl's corpse and started rummaging for the artifact with the head of his weapon.

How do you know all of these things about Zahrellion and Rikky? Jenka asked as he began urging them all to get away from the area. *If I wasn't here that long, you'd have had to leave right after I did.*

We've a new way to travel great distances, March voiced. *You saw Crimzon leave. We can be home in a matter of days.*

They were flying over open sea now. In the distance behind them the dark horizon line was eclipsed by the explosive release of the Soulstone's power when Orthon finally destroyed it.

We should seek shelter in the sea cave and heal each other's wounds as best we can, Aikira suggested. *The dragons can feed there, and we can catch up. Uh… Your Highness.*

Jenka looked at March, and March chuckled, despite the fact his head was swollen to the point of bursting. *Why did you call her Queen Zahrellion?*

Because King Richard gave you the Frontier to rule, King De Swasso, Aikira answered with a mocking grin. *As the mother of your heir, Zahrellion is Queen Regent.*

And that is why these witches want my son?

It has to be, agreed Marcherion.

We will heal and rest. But we won't rest long, said Jenka.

No one cared to disagree.

CHAPTER THIRTY

*H*erald had a hard time staying inconspicuous in Mainsted. He was once the most notorious of the King's Rangers, the hard-assed master who nicked the ear of any training forester who didn't carry his own weight. After the Dragoneers came, he was promoted to High Ranger, and since he was in Mainsted, Midwal, or Three Forks regularly, he was constantly in the public eye. Herald's brother Swineherd raised the hogs that once graced the tables of the wealthier families of the mainland, too. Trying to hide was next to impossible, at least until Linux spelled a pair of modest monks silly and took their hooded robes.

"I feel like a ninny, you fargin' druidoo," Herald complained as they made their way out to a farmhouse where they thought witches might be gathering. "I 'ent got enough arse left to keep the chill off my nards."

The sun had just set, and the lamp Linux stole had very little fuel left in it, so even unshuttered it was as dim as could be.

"You could have worn your britches under the robe, Herald," Linux grinned. "I have the clothes I had on under here, just in case we have to ditch these."

Linux was clearly trying to keep from laughing at him, and that just made Herald all the grumpier. He would have worn his britches under the robe, only the robe was too short by a foot and any passerby would have seen his boots and known he wasn't a monk. He had sandals on his feet and he didn't like that either. The worst part of it was the fact that he didn't have his trusty old sword. The only weapon he was carrying was a long dagger.

"Are you sure Rikky told you of this place?" The farther out of Mainsted they walked, the less confident Herald felt. He hadn't liked the idea of trusting Linux at all, and now he was taking orders through the druid on the faith that he was communicating with the Dragoneers.

"I told you," Linux huffed, "Zahrellion and I are communicating through an ancient druidic spell."

"Bah," Herald snorted. "That is what I don't believe. That girl hates you. You betrayed every fiber of her faith in that mess with your brother."

"She wouldn't bother with me if her son hadn't been taken, I assure you," Linux conceded. "I betrayed myself, too." Linux's head dropped as they paced on down the dirt cart track. "I murdered a man, and then destroyed his reputation while wearing his skin. But that's not nearly the worst of it. For King Richard, I picked through groups of innocents and chose the ones he would next torture and kill. I am not proud of these things, Herald. I am here now trying to help the Dragoneers, trying to help Zahrellion get back her son. I know there is no real redemption for me. I doubt there is anything I could do to right all that wrong, but I will live out my days serving good and hope I can find peace with myself while doing so."

"What will they do with the boy?" Herald asked, shaking off his dislike of the druid for the time. Knowing how much Mysterian had loved Richard, and how far that vile boy had gone, chapped the good half of Herald's arse quite badly. That wasn't the boy he was really concerned about, though. He wanted Jericho home safe as badly as any of them.

"He is the heir to the whole kingdom, unless Richard has a son. I think the witches plan on raising him to suit their will, sort of like Mysterian and the Hazeltine were doing with Richard."

"And Jenka, I suppose." Herald didn't like hearing that truth, but he knew it was so. "Mother De Swasso was a witch, just like the rest of 'em."

"She was." Linux gave him a pat on the shoulder and pointed at the large farmhouse sitting off the road. "But she was really Jenka's mother."

Herald followed Linux's finger. A four-square of illuminated curtains and the partial outline of an ill-seated door could be made out. There were a half-dozen horses tethered to the post beside the place, and as they eased around the building in the darkness they saw a fancy carriage and two wagon carts. The teams were being watched over by a pair of capable-looking uniformed men.

"Are they city guards or mercenaries?" Linux asked in a whisper.

"I can't see their boots from here to tell." Herald squinted as he tried to see them.

"Their boots?" Linux asked.

"If they're city guards or soldiers, them boots'll be polished. If they are sellswords, they'll be well worn."

"Look, there." Linux pointed at the light thrown across the ground from a curtained window on the far side of the place. There were a few people in the room, as indicated by the silhouettes they could see moving about.

"I think we can get under the sill and listen," Herald said, wishing again he had his sword and boots on. "We'll know if they're witches right quickly, I'd guess."

"All right," Linux agreed and started moving that way.

Herald followed, while keeping an eye on the men by the carriage. He still couldn't make out a sheen on their boots, so he was guessing they were hired blades. He had to give his attention to his footfalls, so he didn't bother voicing his opinion. If he and Linux were discovered, they'd have to fight, no matter who the men were.

Even before they were under the sill they could hear a man droning on and on about some troops he commanded. It wasn't until Herald and Linux were situated with their backs to the exterior wall, directly under the window, that they could actually understand what was being said, though.

"… taking control of the wall, as I just said, will be the easiest part of it." The man spoke with confidence and authority. "I don't think attacking the Frontier towns will be effective unless we control the wall. It's just not—"

"You are not here to think so much, my dear," a seductive female voice responded. "We already control Mainsted Harbor, and my girls are in Port charming the workers to our will as we speak. The Frontier's coin comes from the goods they ship to the Nightshade and my pet king."

Hearing that caused Herald to turn and try to peek into the room. He inched his head up and found just enough parting in the curtains to see inside. There was a table, and down its length were the remains of what must have been a healthy feast. At the head of the board, sitting in a throne-like chair, was a man wearing the uniform of a kingdom commander, and sitting in his lap was the witch Ankha Vira.

Herald immediately dropped back down beside Linux. "She's here, druid. Get a spell ready. We have surprise on our side. You can zap her right through the window."

"Let me see." Linux turned and looked for himself. "We don't know where the baby is yet."

Herald popped up beside him, and, like two adolescent boys, they jostled for a view.

"The wall is but a symbol, my handsome man," Ankha Vira's hands were roaming the commander's chest now. His eyes were half-lidded, and he looked to be deep in his cups. "What purpose does the barrier serve now?"

"None, since the Dragoneers rid the land of its vermin," he responded.

"Mighty Garrin Fedran, Lord of the Mainland, right hand to King Jericho. How does that sound, dear?" She was practically purring into his ear.

"Much better than Commander Fedran of King Richard's forgotten lands."

"Then get your men in position to march through the Midwal gate. They will ride in the darkness to Three Forks and attack with the first light of day. You've only a few days to manage this, love. Can you do it?"

"But what of Outwal?" the commander asked as he nodded that he could.

"The men of Port will take care of the ones my girls don't sway first." She kissed his ear and Linux slid back down. Herald waited only a moment to join him.

"They are planning to wage war against the people of the Frontier," said Linux. "I have to warn Zahre—"

Herald would have asked Linux what he was trying to say, but both of them were suddenly gagged. Herald tried to pull whatever had covered his mouth away from his face, but sparkling yellow ropes formed of magical energy had snaked around his wrists and ankles, too. A witch stepped up out of the darkness and clucked at them. On either side of her was some sort of dog-sized insect-looking thing. Her hellish creatures had amber, glowing eyes and looked like they could rip a man to shreds in a matter of seconds.

Herald didn't even think of trying to escape. If he'd had britches on, he'd have been worried about shitting them.

CHAPTER THIRTY-ONE

"Linux said the bitch was there, but they never saw or heard where Jericho was," Zahrellion said. Her cool was quickly evaporating. She wasn't sure how she'd kept it together this long. Knowing Jericho was in the hands of that witch was maddening at best. Her only hope was that Ankha Vira wanted to keep him alive, not kill him. "They don't know where they are being taken, but at least Linux can communicate with me."

The two Dragoneers were sitting at a map table in the Midwal keep the Coven Wisteria had been using. A pair of oil lanterns hung on ensconced hooks, and the musty smell of some old brew was in the air. It was a crowded space, but no one seemed to notice. There was too much else going on.

Rikky had eaten most of the food brought to them, but Zahrellion couldn't muster an appetite.

Only after she indicated that she wasn't going to finish off the remaining stuff did he wolf it down.

The dragons had fed and were now resting. They would be ready to fly at a moment's notice. Crystal was only resting so that she could better manifest her anger later. If she'd had her way, they would be glacializing the peninsula one building at a time until Prince Jericho was safe. Zah wasn't sure why she wasn't as eager, but her reservations were fading. The witches wouldn't hurt the baby physically, not if they intended to use him, or ransom him, but they could do terrible mental damage.

Zahrellion had Keepers riding all over the mainland to round up men willing to help them. Before holing into his Kingston palace, King Richard had proclaimed quite clearly to all that Zahrellion commanded nothing on his side of the wall. This made it hard to gather support, and even harder to get information. Luckily, the Frontier was ripe with resources, and Jericho's coffers were full. Her men had to use coins to buy whatever information they could. No one, however, knew where baby Jericho had been taken. That meant Zahrellion couldn't act with any measure of confidence.

The best map of the Frontier, unrolled over the sectional maps, was old and didn't have any of the sprouting, smaller villages marked on it. It wasn't helping. All it did was serve to remind Zah how far away her son could be by now. She didn't know what she would do if she didn't get him back. First she'd lost Jenka, then Aikira, and now her son. It was all too much to take.

"I need to get Herald before something happens to him," Rikky said. "I have a bad feeling about it. I'd bet my last copper that Jericho is there somewhere. Linux said it himself. The witches hold the harbor, and whoever holds the harbor holds the city. It is the safest place for them to keep him."

"Rikky, these are witches, not sensible people." The harsh snap of Zahrellion's voice made Rikky blanch, and she quickly softened her tone. She'd already caused Aikira to run off with her unrestrained mouth.

Oh, how she wanted her best friend back.

Rikky was dearest to her, but he wasn't a girl and couldn't understand much. She'd taken for granted Aikira's kindness and abused her position, if only subtly, but that was enough. She'd been wrong, and she didn't dare hurt another friend, especially brave little Rikky who would willingly lay down his life for her.

"You are probably right, but they could have—most likely do have—another place of gathering. No one can so much as say when and where they started. They've more numbers than I could imagine."

"I've been thinking about that," Rikky said. "When I was seeing Rosalia in Farwal, she commented once on how sad all the fatherless children must be. A whole bunch of kingdom men died fighting Gravelbone and his hordes, then that other thing nearly destroyed the Outlands. There are hundreds and hundreds of wives and mothers left without."

"A roof and warm food would have brought most of them right into the fold," Zahrellion agreed. "None of this speculation is helping us find him, though, Rikky!"

"I know." Rikky reached over and gave her a sincere hug. "I have to go get Herald, Zah. If Jericho is there, I will bring him back to you."

"I'm going with you." She hugged him back. "I have a feeling you are right. Jericho will most likely be wherever they are taking Herald and Linux."

"That's the Zahrellion I know," said Rikky. "Let's go get your son."

* * *

Even bound by magical ropes and bouncing along beside Herald in a cart, Linux felt a bit more at ease with his life than he had before Rikky spotted him in the streets of Mainsted. He wasn't a bad person, didn't ever intend to be one. In fact, he could argue that if it weren't for him, the Dragoneers would have never been.

Linux was the one who helped Zahrellion find the other Dragoneers and warn King Blanchard of Gravelbone's attack. He had done many things that could, in his mind, justify killing Rolph. The man's life hadn't been wasted at all. But Linux was also the one who'd chosen the people Richard tortured and killed. He hadn't had much choice, but he could have fled sooner than he did. Knowing what Richard was about gave him another chance at redemption.

Zahrellion had to know about the boy's sick atrocities. Something had to be done. To him, this witchy mess was just an obstacle to overcome. He'd seen Zahrellion angry. He had been her mentor and had trained and taught her to use the Dour. He didn't think these witches understood what they were dealing with. He didn't think the upstart coven had half a chance, at least until they got where they were going. Then something happened that changed his perception completely.

The wagon came to a jostling halt and the blanket that had been covering them was thrown off. Herald's robe had ridden up his body, and he was as exposed as he was angry at the way they were being treated. They were forced to sit up, hands behind their backs, feet dangling from the rear of the wagon as if it were a bench.

They were near an open barn. Torches were staked into the earth on either side of them, but their wavering orange illumination revealed very little. They could have been anywhere, but Linux could smell the brine and knew they were near the sea. One of the men there used the tip of his sword to get Herald's robe back over his knees, but a high-pitched wail resounded and everyone fled the scene as if death himself was coming.

There were a few moments of ruffling and then the decided thump of something large stepping near.

"Linux, you disappoint me," said a voice that froze Linux's heart.

It was King Richard striding into the light. The Nightshade was rising up behind him menacingly, its cherry eyes showing its restrained eagerness to strike if ordered to do so.

"You disappoint *me,* you fargin' rotten excuse for a shit sack!" The vehemence with which Herald spoke was as surprising as finding Richard mixed up in all this madness. "Mysterian loved you, raised you to be good, and you broke her heart."

"Mysterian is dead, old man!" Richard shot back. "She was no different than any other witch. You would kill Ankha for taking my nephew from his mother, yet you loved that old whore after she took Jenka from his."

King Richard looked every bit the dark, nasty ruler he'd become, with dull black armor and a wicked-looking jagged-edged blade. His eyes were a shade blacker than the deep circles under them, and his complexion was pale. He spat between them and then stepped up so he could look Herald in the eye. "Out of respect for your reputation and years of service to my father, I will not prolong your death." With that, he backhanded Linux off of the wagon and walked away.

Linux watched helplessly as the Nightshade snaked its sinuous neck down and snapped Herald into its jaws.

Herald struggled, but the magical binds holding him wouldn't let him break free. He didn't make a sound as he was crushed, chewed, and swallowed in one sloppy gulp.

Linux couldn't keep from vomiting, but emptying his stomach wasn't so much caused by the gore of an old friend's terrible death. It was more because vile King Richard had spoken the truth of it.

He, Mysterian, and Vax Noffa had decided the fate of Richard and Jenka and a hundred others with no concern for who it hurt. Now someone else was trying to do the same thing with another prince.

Half-expecting the Nightshade to eat him next, he did one of the hardest things he had ever done. Through the druidic link he'd established with Zahrellion, he told her of Herald's fate and Richard's involvement. It was all he could do, for he still didn't know where he was, much less where the baby had been taken.

CHAPTER THIRTY-TWO

Zahrellion knew she couldn't catch Rikky now. Not only was it so dark and cloudy that they couldn't see more than a few hundred yards ahead of them, but Silva was far too fast for Crystal to keep pace with. They were speeding in a blind rage toward Mainsted. Zahrellion had been following them, pleading with them to stand down and think before rushing in, but once she'd told Rikky of Herald's death, the boy's eyes narrowed and he became something that frightened her.

She'd never seen the expression, but Jenka had, and he'd tried to explain it to her once while they made small talk from their pillows. Jenka had said that once Rikky decided he was going to kill Gravelbone, he became something else.

"Not actually something else?" she'd asked.

"No, my love. He just stops being aloof little Rikky and becomes a force of determination not to be reckoned with. Sort of like when he first lost his leg. He had a peg leg fitted while it was all still raw and tender."

Rikky was like that now, and no matter how hard Zahrellion pleaded with him in the ethereal, he refused to respond. She doubted he was even listening to her anymore. Silva wasn't responding, either, not even to Crystal, which had never happened before. Zahrellion wasn't sure if he'd heard that Ankha Vira and her witches weren't who killed Herald. She didn't get to finish telling him the whole of what Linux had told her. She wasn't sure if he understood that this meant war had been declared against them, and she was going to have to return to Three Forks and rally what people and troops she could muster to fight. All she could hope was that he didn't run off and get himself or Jericho killed.

Turning away from the chase was one of the hardest things she ever had to do. She wanted more than anyone alive to race in and rescue Jericho while delivering revenge for Herald, but that just couldn't be. She was the Queen of the Frontier and she had people to protect. She'd learned the lesson of responsibility at the cost of a few hundred soldiers' lives once. She wouldn't sacrifice the people for the prince. That wasn't how true royalty was supposed to rule. She had to help the people defend themselves, at the very least. If troops were coming through the Midwal Gate, then she needed to surprise them.

It churned her stomach to think so, but she was almost glad Linux was helping inform her. He'd been a fantastic teacher, and up until he soul-stepped King Blanchard, he'd been more or less her idol. The fact that he'd asked her for forgiveness while telling her of Herald's fate wasn't lost on her. Maybe, after her son, and now Rikky were back safe, she could grant it. Until then Linux would just be what he was, a murderous spy who wanted her favor back. Right now she had to focus.

With a grim set to her jaw and an expression not unlike Rikky's, she turned Crystal around and started getting her mind ready for a war that was undoubtedly going to break her heart. As a mother, she was terrified for her son, but as his Queen Regent, she was ready to end this madness with a bloodbath and unify the lands for him.

***

In the early morning, Rikky brought Silva down right on the farmhouse where Herald and Linux had overheard the witches' plan. The prisoners who'd told them of the coven's place had detailed its location well enough that it was easy for him to find from the sky. The pewter-colored wyrm sprayed molten liquid breath all over the tiled roof, and as the stuff cooled and hardened into its soft metallic state, the weight collapsed the rafters. The first woman who came running out was wearing the clothes of a servant girl, and Silva spared her, but the second came out blowing a ball of fire up at them, and Rikky's Dour-formed arrow tore right through her leg. The whole structure crumbled then, and three witches came racing out of the pile of dust and debris on their brooms.

Silva snapped up one of them and then slung the resulting limp body away from her.

A fireball lit up the morning before it impacted them, and though they were engulfed in an explosion of flames, they were not badly injured, for Rikky had previously cast a shielding to protect them from the novices' crude castings.

"Tell me where they have taken Prince Jericho and we will spare your lives," Rikky commanded. "If you don't, you are soon to die."

One of the witches spat at them. She was instantly bathed in boiling hot spew and falling.

She ended up crumpling into a hardened fetal knot on the ground.

The last of them tried to dart away on her broomstick, but Silva's speed kept her from going far.

"Last chance," Rikky called.

"They'll kill me if I tell you," the witch said. In the bright light of dawn Rikky realized she was but a girl, not much older than he was. She looked terrified, fidgeting around in the air on her wobbly stick.

"I'll kill you if you don't," came Rikky's reply.

"I'll tell you," the older witch, who had her leg nearly removed by Rikky's magical arrow, said from the ground.

"Don't tell him," the broom rider called. "She won't forgive you if you do."

"None of us knows where Ankha Vira has taken the baby, but I know where they took those two men they caught snooping."

"Where?" Rikky asked sharply. "Tell me or I'll kill you both."

CHAPTER THIRTY-THREE

Zahrellion realized a moment too late that she and Crystal weren't alone in the sky. Crystal knew exactly when Zah did, and the fact that they'd been surprised angered them both. It was too late to chastise themselves, though, for here came a half-dozen witches of the more capable sort, all cackling and merry as they started flying circles around the large frost dragon.

Crystal tried to snatch one of them but missed. Zahrellion had a spell on the tip of her tongue, but just as she was about to speak the word that released a powerful pulse of Dour, she saw Ankha Vira. The witch had baby Jericho in her arms, and a long, black fingernail that was tipped with a sharpened steel extension was against his temple.

"I don't really need him, you know," the witch hissed. "Richard's seed is potent enough to create an heir inside me, and I am clever enough to get into his bed as I please."

"Not even that lunatic would stoop so low as to bed you," Zahrellion spat.

Ankha Vira laughed. "Oh dear, but you are wrong. His will is the only reason your son isn't in my brewing kettle as it is. Gravelbone left the king vulnerable, and he needed someone, a bosom to bury his face in, if you will. How could he resist mine?" She pushed out her ample chest proudly. "You will be coming with us now. There is no need to put up a struggle. Young Rikky Camille is finding himself in a similar situation to yours, and we will kill him and Jericho both if you do not comply. King Richard wants to speak with you. I give him what he wants now."

"I thought you wanted to rebuild the Council of Three? I thought you wanted the kingdom as it had been?"

"That was before I tasted Richard's madness. The pleasure of the pain he offers is exquisite. We will unify the kingdom, and there will be no more need for Dragoneers, or rangers, or even city guards, for the people will serve us with complete loyalty, if only out of fear."

Zahrellion wanted to say that she and Richard were exactly why the Dragoneers were needed, but she bit her tongue. If what the witch was saying were true, then there was no need for them to keep Jericho alive. There was no reason for them to keep her or Rikky alive, either, but she wouldn't just let them kill her. She would use her remaining time to bargain for her son, and hope that she found an opportunity to kill the dark king and his harlot in the process.

* * *

Having warded each other even more as they bolted away from the crumbled farmhouse, Rikky and Silva were aware of the witches trying to surprise them long before they made their move. They were close to Mainsted's outer wall, and closing rapidly. It was clear the witches of the Coven Wisteria had no idea how fast he and Silva could move. None of them expected what the pewter-colored wyrm did next, nor did Rikky. It was all he could do to hold onto his dragon.

Silva slowed until they could see the fastest flying of the witches behind them, then she pulled straight up and back, and within the span of a heartbeat was flying in the opposite direction. Her molten breath launched up into an arcing spray, and though none of the witches were bathed in the stuff, most of them were scalded from the droplets that showered over them as they flew through it.

Rikky urged Silva to dive under them, but his dragon feigned an upward turn before doing so. The maneuver served to make a blown fireball and a spiraling streak of buzzing hornet-like sparkles miss them completely.

Silva went into a dive and Rikky began breathing deeply because he knew he could black out when she leveled off at this speed.

Rikky hadn't had a father, and Jenka had always been like an older brother to him. They'd grown up together in Crag. Master Kember had been killed before Rikky's eyes just moments before Rikky's leg was eaten by goblins. Losing Herald was so painful that he wasn't sure he could stand it. On top of that, he was ashamed that Jericho had been taken from them. He knew Zahrellion was hurting inside, for she loved that baby more than life itself. He knew she didn't like being responsible for all the people of the Frontier, either. The anger helped him cope, and as Rikky focused his aggression, he wished more than anything that he could avenge Herald and get Jericho back for Zah.

As the heavy pull of Silva's deep-curving upturn slipped away, Rikky let all of his emotion loose and took aim. Dour-formed arrow after Dour-formed arrow streaked away from his bow, and in a matter of moments the witches were scattered, two of them tumbling from the sky into the cobbled streets below.

One of the witches had an enchanted bow similar to Rikky's, though he doubted it was sustained by the teardrop of a dragon. Her arrow nicked his flesh, and two more found their way through Silva's scales.

The dragon roared out and turned away, and Rikky had to swallow his heart back down his throat as they nearly crashed full-on into the Nightshade.

A shrieking call cut through the air, and Rikky and the witches were forced to slam their palms against their ears to protect them from the terrible sound.

Silva pulled up and darted away. Then she went into a hover while keeping a defensive posture and a bit of distance from them all. Rikky was amazed at how much Richard had changed. When they fought Gravelbone, he had worn polished steel armor chased with bright blue, the color of Royal's scales. Now his plated mail was dark, as if it had been blackened in a fire. Richard wore a helmet studded all over with finger-long spikes, and his eyes sunk so deep into the visor that they were impossible to see.

After the Nightshade's screech ended, Rikky called across the air a bit more loudly than he needed to. "What are you doing here? Are you here to help me kill these fargin' witches?"

"Fargin' witches?" Richard laughed. "You sound exactly like that fat old bastard I just killed."

"What?" Rikky asked. A wave of confusing nausea washed over him. Around them, the witches were circling at a wary distance.

"Herald Kaljatig," King Richard went on. "I just let my mount here eat him for supper. I should have let him eat Linux, too."

"You!" Rikky screamed with tears welling in his eyes. "You killed Herald? Why would you do such a thing?"

"For the same reason I am going to kill you." Richard rolled his shoulders, as if he knew there was about to be a fight on his hands. "It's really simple. I told you all to stay on your side of the wall and you didn't."

"Me and Zah fought a serpent just to bring back the stuff Mysterian needed to make an antidote after Gravelbone poisoned you. You wouldn't even be alive if it weren't for us."

"I know, Rikky." Richard laughed again. "I just don't care. After Royal died, I learned that there is no good in the world. You and Zahrellion should have let me die. I didn't want to be saved. But since you helped revive me, this is all your fault."

Richard waved a hand sharply, and all of a sudden there was a magically formed net coming down over them. Rikky wasn't sure if the Nightshade or the witches had created it. Either way, Silva's wings were entangled, and now they were falling.

CHAPTER THIRTY-FOUR

Rikky wasn't sure why, but Silva was suddenly able to catch air with her wings. They narrowly missed the rooftops of the buildings just inside Mainsted's great wall, and people were screaming and pointing up from all sections of the city. Rikky caught his breath and turned just in time to see a witch explode into a mist of sparkling bloody ash. Thankfully, Silva avoided flying through the mess.

Rikky saw them then, and he'd never felt so much relief in his life. He also saw the Nightshade carrying King Richard swiftly away from the knot of witches he'd left behind.

Here came Blaze and Jade streaking past Silva. They were chasing after Richard and his hellborn wyrm. And there was Aikira pulverizing another witch with a thrown fist of energy. Two of the three witches were already fleeing, but the third and last of them was gesturing rapidly with the intention of returning Aikira's favor.

Rikky pulled his bow over his shoulder and willed an arrow out of the Dour. It tore through the air but missed the wicked woman. It caused her to lose the spell she was casting, though, which allowed Silva enough time to shower her with molten spew as they passed.

Where is Zah? Aikira voiced when they came around to face Rikky. *What was going on here? Why are you on this side of the wall?*

"You ran off with Marcherion, and a witch stole Jericho!" Rikky screamed as a dam of tears broke. His face was anguished as he finished. "Now Herald is dead, and Richard wants to take over the Frontier. Where have you been?"

By the gods, I'm sorry about Herald, Rikky, Aikira voiced calmly. *Where have they taken the baby? Where is Lemmy?*

The witches got him, Rikky said, trying to get his emotions under control. He was glad Silva was keeping them close to Golden and Aikira. He'd had the thought that he might not see any of them again. *We don't know what they did with Lemmy.*

They spelled one of the coven to look like him and then took Jericho from us.

Aikira looked crestfallen, and Rikky felt a bit of regret for being accusatory when he started explaining.

Where is Zahrellion? she asked.

Rikky wiped a sniffle on his sleeve. *The witches are planning to storm the Midwal gate and attack Three Forks. I'm sure she went to warn them.*

Should we chase down those two witches?

We'd be better to follow them from up high. A spark of hope lifted Rikky's spirits, if only slightly. *Maybe they will lead us to Jericho.*

Agreed.

Then let's go. Rikky urged Silva to climb. *Before they can lose us.*

No need to worry about that. Aikira made a long gesture and then spoke the words to a spell unfamiliar to Rikky. *Just follow Golden through.*

The only thing more amazing than flying into the spinning cylindrical tube forming in the sky was that when they emerged from the other end of the tunnel, the witches were flying directly below them.

That was awesome, Rikky said. *I don't think they've seen us.* He considered his next thought for a moment. *Just because you can get somewhere faster than me, Aikira, doesn't mean Golden is faster than Silva.*

* * *

Marcherion couldn't remember not being angry. Since the day Brendly Tuck died, since the elves more or less forced him into being a Dragoneer, his attitude had been off-kilter toward the aggressive side. After he saw Crimzon fighting the priests with his true rider, March was nothing less than envious. The two were lethal, and awesome to behold. He hoped the two of them found a nice place to wither away, for that is what Clover was doing as she fought. The idea that she was freed from being a statue only to gain all her years back at once seemed unfair. And, as usual, Marcherion was angry about it. When he saw King Richard and the Nightshade laughing as Silva tumbled toward the ground, his rage boiled over.

He burned through the witch's magical netting and then let the cherry red rays burning out of his eye sockets slide across the Nightshade's scaleless hide. When he saw that Silva had caught herself, he let the intense power of the medallion he wore rise up from his chest into his throat. The charge of Dour he vomited forth vaporized one of the witches. King Richard and his hellborn mount used the moment to get some distance, but Jenka and Jade were right behind them. Marcherion and Blaze didn't hesitate to follow.

Get to the right a little, March said into the ethereal. He hardly ever used the ability, but there was no way Jenka would hear him if he yelled.

Yusss. It was Jade who responded, but he saw the corners of Jenka's mouth turn up when Jenka looked back over his shoulder.

Marcherion didn't need motivation, but he thought about little Rikky slamming into the cobbles just the same. The surge of anger that assailed him was potent, and his eye rays were as focused as they'd ever been. When they cut across the Nightshade, they burned right through the wing membrane and actually removed a bit of the tip.

March wasn't expecting the ear-shredding shriek that came in response to the damage, but Jenka apparently wasn't fazed by the sound at all. When Jade darted past and then curved around the big, dark wyrm in an impossible flash of motion, Marcherion was left dumbfounded. Jenka was something beyond human now. It was clear in the way his eyes glowed and the strange aura that clung to him, but seeing him and his dragon move as if the rest of the world were stuck in a jar of molasses was amazing to behold.

Even with all of Jenka's strange power, Richard's blow found him. Jenka and Jade stopped their supernatural burst of movement in the Nightshade's path, and then, as if they were backhanded by some angry god with a club, they were violently pummeled sideways.

Marcherion's anger reached the place where his dragon and the power of the dragon tear medallion took him over. It was a good thing, for had he not been consumed in the rush of Dour-infused battle lust, his defenses might not have been as acute. The pulse of Dour that erupted from his throat missed the dark king, and the Nightshade wasn't affected by Blaze's charring brimstone breath at all.

It was a disheartening pass, but March urged his dragon around for more. He saw that Jenka and Jade were recovering, but then a blast of Richard's magic impacted them and every bit of air, as well most of his thoughts, were knocked from him completely.

CHAPTER THIRTY-FIVE

*J*enka was still reeling from everything Aikira and March had told him about his son. Now Rikky was telling him through the ethereal that Richard, or some witches, had taken Jericho from his mother. All of this came to him while trying to recover from Richard's gut-pulverizing attack. Seeing Marcherion and Blaze hammered across the sky in a similar fashion only served to fuel his determination. He wasn't about to let Richard have the baby he'd yet to see, but only after he saw Blaze recover did he confront his brother.

Do you have him? Jenka yelled with his mind. He could feel his relation to his disturbed brother somehow. He could feel the blood they shared, and he didn't like it.

Ankha Vira has them both, Jenksy. Richard's smile actually looked genuine. *I have to say, I have missed you. Did you save the old red's pet, or whatever you were trying to do?*

If you harm Zahrellion or my son, I will destroy you.

The Nightshade hissed, and Richard laughed disdainfully. *You'll want to destroy me anyway. Besides, I might just destroy you and the Dragonetts first.*

With that, Richard drew his jagged blade and pointed the tip at Jenka. *I'll send you the pieces of Zahrellion when I am done with her, but Jericho has my father's blood in his veins. He will be my heir.*

The alien nature that had infused itself inside Jenka combined with the Dour that saturated his blood. His anger flared forth, and his will carried him and his dragon right into Richard and his hovering mount. Jenka left his saddle and, after slapping Richard's sword out of his hand, he jammed his four fingers into Richard's mouth and closed his fist over his lower jaw.

Richard was still moving at a normal rate, while Jenka and Jade were both acting in some sort of hyper speed. Jade raked a claw down the hellborn wyrm's side, and then Jenka half-hovered, half-strode back over to his own dragon, pulling King Richard with him by the jaw.

He jerked his brother over Jade's saddle like a sack, and just as the effects from the swift of movement spell faded, the green wyrm banked away from the Nightshade. Jade took them straight down to the ground, and a dozen feet above it, Jenka dragged his brother after him. He landed on his feet but had to take a knee as Richard's chest slammed into the dirt. He didn't want to lose his grip just yet.

Jenka rolled his brother over and then put his knee in his chest.

"You'll tell me where Zahrellion and Jericho are or I will rip your face off," Jenka raged while looking deep into Richard's eyes. Every time Richard tried to bite down on his fingers he squeezed his fist tight with just enough force to keep from shattering his jaw bone. Richard's nostrils flared as he struggled to breathe. His eyes were wide with the terror Jenka knew he was radiating.

Richard screamed around Jenka's hand but couldn't use his tongue. Still, Jenka didn't let go. *Are you going to tell me?* he asked with his mind.

They are to be put under Fedran's guard in the Dragoneers' den in Mainsted. The vehemence behind Richard's ethereal voice was plain. *You'll regret ever trying—*

Jenka squeezed his brother's jaw so tightly even his ethereal voice stopped. There was no scale grand enough to measure the amount of fury building inside him now.

You heard him. Jenka craned his neck around, searching the sky for Blaze. The red wyrm and Jade were hovering on either side of the wounded, but still flying, Nightshade. Marcherion was there in his saddle, looking back and forth between the scene on the ground and the slick-skinned wyrm. He looked eager.

Rikky, Aikira, they're on their way to Mainsted. Intercept them, Jenka voiced with his mind.

Them? came Rikky's reply.

The witch has Zahrellion, too, Marcherion responded to the others. Then to Jenka: *Kill him. Let's go get Zah and Jericho back.*

Jenka took a long look at the dark king and groaned out a roar of frustration. *I can't kill him.*

Why not? Marcherion asked.

He is my brother, Jenka huffed. *That's why.*

Just then the Nightshade tried to lift and bank away, but Jade blocked its path and Marcherion urged Blaze to attack.

In savage fashion, the red dragon opened his maw, and when the hellborn wyrm made to protect itself from his fire, Blaze took a huge bite out of the thing instead.

Jade snapped his head in and took a bite as well. His teeth caught bone, and he crunched right through a wing member. The Nightshade went spinning, slowly at first, and impacted into the dirt near Richard and Jenka.

"NOOOO!" Richard yelled as he bucked and kicked Jenka back. Had he not just seen the troublesome beast wounded almost directly over his head, Jenka might not have let his brother go, but now Richard was back-crabbing to get some distance, and before anyone could react, he was running toward the floundering creature and keening out an angry wail of what might have been sorrow.

Jenka leapt from the ground. He covered the sixty-some-odd paces between him and his dragon in a sudden flash of movement.

Mainsted, was all he said as he urged Jade in the right direction. As soon as Blaze was caught up to them, Jenka cast a spell that teleported them all right into the old dragon bailey where they and their mounts had once lived as the heroes of the realm.

PART IV
RETURN OF THE EMERALD RIDER

CHAPTER THIRTY-SIX

Zahrellion saw Jenka as she was shoved into the dark hall that led to the gathering room where they once held council. Her heart leapt with a thundering of hope. If Jenka and Jade were here, maybe the others were, too. She was flooded with relief until she bumped into something warm and fleshy. Then, in a panic, she cast forth an orb of light and was completely surprised that her magic responded to her. What she saw under the harsh, hissing illumination made her retch. Hanging from the rafters by his wrists, with his feet a foot off the ground, was Rolph. It was Linux in Rolph's body, she knew, and he was covered with welts and bruises. What caused her stomach to turn, though, was the dangling finger-wide strips of flesh someone had peeled partially down his ribs.

Zahrellion was suddenly afraid for her son. Jenka might not know he was taken. She was worried for Crystal, too. The huge frost dragon had been backed into one of the dragon stalls and collared with some witchy device that sapped her will.

A groan escaped the hanging form, and Zah forced her worry away long enough to cast the few healing spells she knew on him. Fighting nausea and revulsion, she used a table knife to cut away the dangling strips of drying skin and healed over the raw spots as best she could.

Outside, a commotion was causing men to shout and start clanging around in their armor.

Linux wasn't conscious, which was for the best. Had he been, the pain would have been excruciating. He was lying on his chest now, on the cold tile floor. He had a fever and was fidgeting fitfully but would probably recover.

After she caught her breath, she tried to reach out to her dragon, but there was no response. She tried calling the other Dragoneers with her ethereal voice, too, but no one replied. As she was trying to recall the layout of this part of the castle, she remembered something Rikky had once shown her.

Again hope filled her, for the secret panel that led directly to King Blanchard's old study was still there. After opening it, she gave Linux's still form a glance. He'd taught her most everything she knew, including that you couldn't trust everyone, and that sometimes bad things are done for good reasons.

She maintained that thought as she extinguished her magical light and made her way into the passage. If any of the city guard tried to stop her, she would do her best not to harm them. They were not evil, like Richard and the witch; they were just following Commander Fedran's orders.

As she went, she began thinking through her catalogue of spells for ones that could stop the men without killing them. She remembered a few, but soon something else stole her attention.

They touched her face first and then she felt the spider webs she was breaking through coming down as if a net had fallen on her. The thump of something landing on her shoulder caused her to let out a little scream. She started running with one hand in front of her and the other brushing awkwardly at her head and shoulders. Even after she was sure the thing was off of her, she felt all creepy and on edge. Thankfully, she saw the rectangular outline of the door to the old king's study and eased up to listen to what might be transpiring in the room.

"Who ordered it?" a man asked incredulously. "I do not like this at all."

"The commander is leading the men through the wall. Ankha Vira had us put her in with that traitor."

"She is a Dragoneer, man," the first voice said. "She won't just stay in there. The others have come for her already. They saved us all, and now look at what that fool is—"

"That fool and the witch, as well as King Richard himself, are about to meet their end," Zahrellion said sharply as she burst into the room. Both men cowered in fear, for they'd been there when the Royal Dragoneers defeated Gravelbone. Now their commander had men battling her fellow dragon riders from the wall tops. "I'll not harm you for following the orders you've been given," Zahrellion reassured them, "but I'm giving the orders now." She glared daggers at them until they both nodded that they understood.

"Where is my son?"

"Son?" the first man, a captain, asked.

"The witch took Prince Jericho. Where is he? Where is my son?"

Both men blanched from her angry tone, but it was clear they didn't know what she was talking about. They had no idea where Jericho was.

"What would you have us do?" the second man, a sergeant, finally asked. He looked at his captain and then back at Zah.

"Round up all the men loyal to the Dragoneers. Remind them that they've been forgotten by their king. Tell them that if they fight for King Richard, or that witch, we will kill them. If they fight with us, the transgressions of the past few years will be forgotten."

"But Commander Fedran will—"

"The Dragoneers are here, man, and Commander Fedran is as good as dead. Now go and start spreading the word. The Dragoneers are coming, and they are going to make our kingdom whole again. And any man who can tell me where my son is will earn a purse he'll need a cart to haul for it."

The captain smacked his lips and then nodded. "You heard her, Kildigger. Go tell the men to spread the word."

After the sergeant left, the captain stood and put his hands on his hips. "Those witches guarding over your dragon will know where the prince has been taken. Put this on, and I'll take you right to them."

"Now we are getting somewhere," Zah muttered as she donned the cloak she was given. "Take me directly to whoever has been giving you orders in Fedran's absence."

"I can do that."

CHAPTER THIRTY-SEVEN

Jenka urged Jade up away from the dragon bailey and found March circling higher. Below, men were hesitantly preparing for a battle they didn't look like they wanted to fight. Already, a knot of broom-riding witches was forming to meet the two Dragoneers in the afternoon sky. Another cluster of them was excitedly scurrying about the area around the old dragon barn. Jenka knew that if Zahrellion and Crystal were here, the dragon would have to be held in there.

He used his alien-born ability and the Dour flowing through him to try to sense the frigid wyrm, and he found he was right. Something Richard had said, about Jericho sharing their father's blood, came to him then, too, and he instantly knew his son wasn't in Mainsted. After a few more moments of concentrating on the feeling he'd had when he was near Richard, he decided that Jericho was some distance east of Mainsted. He could feel his own blood as plainly as he could feel that of his father flowing in his brother.

The witches were throwing spells now, but Jenka absently called the Dour to shield him, and their spiraling swarms of angry magic and pitiful fireballs all exploded on a spherical field a few dozen feet before his wyrm.

Marcherion was under attack as well, but Blaze was impervious to the fireballs and actually caught one in his huge toothy maw before spitting it like a melon seed back at the witch who'd cast it.

Jenka called forth a mass of raw Dour and let it float away from him. After warning Marcherion and Blaze, Jade banked them away.

I'm going after my son. I can sense where he is now.

There are too many witches for us to handle alone.

Cover your ears, Jenka voiced.

His hovering mass of Dour exploded then, sending a ring of energy blasting outward at a slightly canted angle nearly parallel to the ground. The concussion caused a handful of the witches to simply fall from the sky, while a few others were knocked backward with violent force. Others were bleeding from their ear holes or outright deafened by the sound.

Where there had just been two dozen of the broom riders in the sky, there were now less than ten.

To the surprise of both Dragoneers, in the stark silence that followed the blast, a few cheers erupted from the men in the city below.

Not too many for you now, are there? Jenka asked, and then he and Jade were but an emerald blur streaking across the sky.

* * *

Marcherion started into the aerial fight by letting Blaze have his head and firing arrows from his bow. This was effective as March was an ace shot with the weapon, and Blaze's breath was noxious and deadly hot. Loosing arrows required a cool demeanor, though, and after one of the spiraling hornet sparkles hit him and seared its way into his shoulder, his aim was off and his anger took over.

The dragon tear medallion at his neck flared cherry, and his eyes began to fill with radiant light. More witches were in the sky now, but he didn't care. The string-thin lines of light burning out of his pupils sliced through everything they touched. First a broom was ruined, leaving the rider flailing as she crashed into the street. Then he cut one of the witches in half and the attack intensified.

One witch arced in and cast some sort of glacial spell that caused Blaze to begin coughing and fighting for purchase in the now icy air.

Another slung liquid across the fire dragon's scales. The stuff did nothing at first, but then blisters were bubbling up and smoky corrosion was eating into his flesh. March was splattered, too, and it felt like scalding oil was on him, pocking his skin.

He saw a broom rider cut under Blaze's spewing flames and knew she was no novice. The woman was older than anyone he'd ever seen, save for maybe Clover when he'd last seen her. She had a flask in her free fist, and she pulled the stopper with her teeth. She didn't sling it, though; she drank it down. Her eyes bulged almost completely out of her old head, but then she blew out a huge swath of icy, wet moisture.

Blaze roared out in agony. March wasn't sure if they were about to crash into the ground or not, but he knew his dragon was struggling to stay aloft. Then, out of the corner of his eye, he saw a flash of gold and silver.

There is a lake in the merchants' quarter, Rikky called across the ethereal. *Get there now!*

March understood that he and Blaze needed to wash the acidic liquid off of them. The way Rikky spoke told him the stuff was doing terrible damage to them both. For a fire drake to want to be in water was a rare thing, but Blaze would have wallowed in slush if it would end the corrosion of his scales.

Once Rikky and Aikira engaged the witches, Blaze got out of the thick of it. On their way down into the park pond, which Rikky had described as a lake, they saw something that was staggering enough to make them forget the agony of their wounds.

"Mudgesss," Blaze hissed distastefully.

When they hit the water and steam started roiling from Blaze's heat, March quickly dove off of the wyrm and swam underwater while rubbing his arms. When he came up for air, he was bleeding and deeply pocked in some places, but the pain was ebbing. One of his eyes was a blurry mess, but he was otherwise intact.

He looked up, hoping his good eye had been deceiving him, but the evening sky was filling with mudged dragons, and the witches clearly had their favor.

March knew they should have killed Richard when they had the chance. They were about to be paying the price for not doing so. The Nightshade had always been able to rally the lesser wyrms, and now here they were. Maybe it wasn't dead, or maybe it was Richard, not the black wyrm, who could call them to battle. It really didn't matter. Someone or something had summoned them.

There must have been a hundred of them, too many to count. March knew the fight was about to be on them, and he and Blaze were still floundering in a pond.

He took in Blaze's injuries and was heartened to see that, like his own, the pain was fading and the wounds weren't deadly. There were a few melon-sized scallops eaten out of the dragon, but he was ready to get back into the sky.

The mudged are coming, Marcherion warned Rikky and Aikira. *Watch yourselves.*

When Blaze lifted up, they flew a few dozen wing strokes toward the battle, but the big red tumbled back to the ground. He was so affected by all the cold and water that he couldn't maintain his equilibrium. As they stumbled to a stop, two mudged dragons came flapping down over them. Blaze let loose a blast of dragon fire, as much to drive them back as to warm up his muscles. Then another mudged wyrm, this one of a deep blue hue speckled with turquoise and orange down its spine, darted its head in and snapped at him. March's left eye was so blurred that he didn't see it coming until it was there. The next thing he knew, he was being dragged out of the saddle by his hair.

CHAPTER THIRTY-EIGHT

Rikky heard Marcherion's warning and glanced at Aikira, who was flying beside them, to see if she'd heard. Aikira gave him a smiling snarl and pointed at the darkened cloud of wyrms in the sky.

Go after the witches, Rikky, she voiced. *Cover March. Golden has a spell for the mudged that you'll want to be clear of.*

Silva called forth a shielding spell for her rider and then banked away. They corkscrewed between the sparkling swirls cast by one of the witches, only to narrowly miss a yellow, glowing net formed of witchy magic cast by another. Then Silva unleashed her spew while Rikky loosed Dour-formed arrow after Dour-formed arrow across the sky at them.

The brooms the witches rode looked more like branches, and most of the riders could maneuver them well enough to avoid his attack, but not all.

One of his arrows hit a witch in the chest, and a film of harsh, rapidly spreading energy crackled over her as she fell backward off of her flying device. Another of them was left with a fist-sized hole through her middle. Rikky guessed that the effect of each of his Dour-formed arrows was different because the witches were each warded differently. Most of the time the missiles struck and exploded out for an instant then sucked back in on themselves, leaving nothing but empty space where the target had been.

Hold on! Aikira yelled.

Golden's spell sent a concussive wave through the sky. There wasn't much sound to it, but the gassy fumes and jagged streaks of substance that exploded out in a growing sphere caused at least two dozen of the inbred wyrms to go tumbling, spinning, or flailing out of the sky.

The wing of a mudged wyrm thumped and grated across Rikky's head, the rough scales peeling his skin from his scalp. Rikky's bow was falling, and his vision was washed over with his own blood. The next thing he knew, the flying vermin were clearing a circle in the sky over the dragon bailey. The dozen or so remaining witches were circling the space, and the mudged were hovering eagerly outside the pattern they were flying.

Rikky searched the area, wondering what had happened to Aikira. He wiped some of the blood from his face with the back of his hand and found that Golden was near him. Aikira was charred across one side of her body and staring intently down at something in the middle of the open circle of sky. It was Marcherion, and he was being dangled by his hair by a partially mudged wyrm of one of the bluer strains. Standing before and slightly under the dragon was the most beautiful woman Rikky had ever seen, while all around the open dragon bailey the walls and rooftops were speckled with people, some archers, and some just wanting to see the Dragoneers do battle.

Ankha Vira was wearing a flowing black dress. The material went around the back of her neck in a bunch and flowed over the front of her with her raven black hair. Her breasts were full and round, and only her nipples were covered by the straps of material that trailed over them and buckled into her girdle. Her eyes were as deep as wells, and her lips as red as cherry juice. She was gesturing upward, and had Rikky not been forced to wipe more blood from his face to see, he might have remained under her charm.

As his vision partially cleared, he realized she was about to do something to Marcherion. Blaze was circling the scene well below the witches and mudged wyrms, but he was clearly afraid to attack for fear of what would happen to his bond-mate.

Before the witch could finish her casting, a couple of people came running up toward them from the building in which they used to gather. Rikky had to strain to hear them.

"Wait!" one of the people, a man in uniform, was calling. "This one has imperative news for you or Commander Fedran."

Ankha Vira's rage was clear in her expression, but she turned nonetheless. The man, a ranking officer of the city guard, Rikky recognized from the uniform, started hesitantly, motioning at the hooded figure beside him.

"What is this, Captain?" Ankha Vira snapped. "I am in no mood for foolery."

"This is no foolery," the hooded figure said and stepped forward, jabbing a blade right through the witch.

Ankha Vira exhaled sharply and her breath blew the hood off of the person, but Rikky already knew by her voice that it was Zahrellion.

Apparently, the witch wasn't fazed by the wound, for she laughed and backhanded Zahrellion to the dirt. During the motion, her image flickered, and Rikky realized that Ankha Vira wasn't really there. How she had managed to create a kinetic blow to Zah, he didn't know, but the act spoke of the true power she might have at her command.

"That does it, little queeny." Ankha Vira reached to the side, her hands disappearing completely as she grabbed something up in them. When she was fully visible again, baby Jericho was in her arms, crying. "Now you can watch helplessly as I kill your child and drink his blood."

"Why would you do such a thing?" Zahrellion dropped the sword and struggled to get to her knees.

"Because consuming him will make the prince soon to be growing inside of me that much stronger." She laughed at them, taking the time to eye Rikky and Aikira hovering on their dragons in the open space above her. She didn't seem concerned with them as she put her long, blade-extended fingernail against the baby's throat.

Oh no, Aikira voiced.

Rikky knew they could do nothing if the witch wasn't actually there with them, and it was all he could bear to see Zahrellion on her knees pleading for the life of her son with her tears.

"Ugggggh," Marcherion yelled as he fell the few feet to the ground. The blue mudged lifted suddenly, with just a clump of tangled brown hair in its claw. March was holding his dagger in one hand and rubbing his scalp with the other. He'd knifed through his own hair to break away and was now stumbling to Zahrellion's side.

"I've had enough of this," Ankha Vira growled. "Let the sacrifice of this child stand as a warning to all you Dragoneers. The time of the witch has come."

Baby Jericho screamed as loud as his mother did when the razor sharp steel slid across his throat.

CHAPTER THIRTY-NINE

*J*enka was pleased that the witch thought she was in control.

He found them at a farmhouse nearer to Midwal than Mainsted. He teleported himself from Jade's back directly to the doorstep. The sea of Dour he was floating in was thick and deep. He was able to sizzle the witch that opened the door to death with a touch to her forehead, and then he was striding toward the sudden screaming sound of his son.

Ankha Vira was there in a large, open room, standing in a circle of burning black candles. A star was lined on the plank wood floor with some white powder, and where the seven tips of the symbol met the circle a larger red candle was burning. The air around the witch seemed different, and as he crept around her he saw Zahrellion's anguished face and the rage exploding across Marcherion's. When he saw his son for the very first time he was forced to hold back the tidal wave of fatherly love and longing that threatened to burst forth. The witch's bladed nail was slicing into the helpless baby's neck, and he had to act.

The surge of alien strength and the volume of raw Dour that accompanied Jenka's kicking boot as it lifted and rocketed up under the witch's ear was only slightly more amazing than the speed with which he snatched his son from the suddenly flailing woman.

Ankha Vira's head impacted the rafters of the farmhouse, and the rest of her body followed. As she fell to the planked floor in a heap, her flowing dress caught fire in the candle flame.

Jenka stepped into the spell circle, cradling his son, and saw the relief spread across Zahrellion's beautiful face. He still couldn't get over how much different she looked without the tattoos on her cheeks and forehead.

"Oh, Jenka De Swasso, you always take my breath away. Is he all right?"

Jenka held his son out and looked at him. The baby had gone surprisingly calm in his arms and was now only sniffling and fussy. There was a deep slice at the corner of his neck under the ear, but Jenka's saturated power was already healing it over. He wanted to say a million things. He wanted to tell Zahrellion how beautiful the life they'd created was. He wanted to savor this moment as long as he lived, but beyond his son's gleaming eyes he saw the numbers of mudged and the confused witches now coming down out of the sky at Zahrellion and March. Then he saw his brother's raging form, riding the back of the blackest mudged wyrm Jenka had ever seen.

"Get him, Marcherion." Jenka looked into his friend's eyes deeply. Then turning to Zahrellion, he met her lavender orbs and saw all the love in the world pooling in them.

"He is beautiful." Jenka smiled for the first time in what seemed like forever. "He is safe now. Let us end this madness so he can grow up in a world full of peace and love."

"You are the hero of my life, Jenka." Zahrellion's glowing smile faded into a grim line of determination. "Take him to Clover's castle and guard over him. We will finish this today." With that, Zahrellion turned and stormed away, leaving Marcherion grinning with delight.

"Make sure the witch is dead," Marcherion said as he followed Zahrellion out of his vision.

Jenka sat Jericho in a cradle, and then he pulled the blade Mysterian had made for him so long ago and relieved the nasty witch of her head.

For good measure, he blasted the woman's body into a pulpy mess and set the rest of the place on fire. He then carried his son onto his dragon, situated him in his lap and urged Jade to fly. When Jade took back to the sky, Jenka had a feeling that from that moment on his life was going to be as wonderful as it ever had been. It didn't matter that he was so much different than them all. Even better, the gleam of wonder in the baby's eyes held all the promise in the world.

* * *

Zahrellion, Rikky, Aikira, and Marcherion started tearing through the remaining witches and mudged over Mainsted with a determined fury. A Dour-formed arrow exploded into an inbred dragon and then collapsed back in on itself, leaving nothing but empty sky.

A swath of dragon breath, followed by three scorching rays of cherry power, seared through the air splitting brooms, witches, and mudged dragon flesh as it went.

Golden liquid spewed forth, and powerful fists of wizardly force smashed into the enemy from seemingly nowhere, while Zahrellion and her dragon glacialized everything that fell from the sky so that it exploded into a million chips of icy gore when it impacted.

There was only the slightest bit of retaliatory attack, mostly because there was no one there to order any of the combatants. The Dragoneers didn't watch the enemy flee, though. Most of those who ran were chased down and ended, until only the Dragoneers remained in the dusky sky.

The people below cheered the victory as mightily as they'd cheered the defeat of Gravelbone. And for the first time as Dragoneers, Marcherion and Aikira were able to feel that sort of glory. Needless to say, both of them relished the moment.

* * *

King Richard's mudged wyrm didn't fly as well as the Nightshade had, nor did it have even a smidgen of the hellborn creature's ability. The mudged responded to his will, but not as diligently or smoothly as they had when he'd commanded them through the Nightshade. Luckily for him, the Nightshade hadn't died in the earlier melee, but it was far too wounded to fly. In fact, it might not ever fly again, but it was alive.

Seeing the battle around him slowly turn in the favor of the Dragoneers compelled him to retreat to the safety of his island stronghold. He didn't care about the mainland anyway. Ankha Vira and her witchy charm had induced him to meet her every desire. It was she who'd desired the power of rule.

Another time, Dark King, the Nightshade said to him through a link not unlike the ethereal. Theirs was a bond of a darker sort, and there would be another day. He knew that losing control of the mainland ports meant the islands would be at the mercy of Queen Zah, or maybe Jenka now, but they wouldn't let the masses starve just to hurt him. In fact, if Jenka couldn't kill him, he didn't figure any of the Dragoneers would try.

It was with reluctance that he called the mudged away from the battle. They too might be needed in the future. They'd definitely be needed to protect him in his island palace. He urged the wyrm he was on to take him back to the Nightshade. He'd learned healing spells while studying under Mysterian when he was but a boy. That thought only made him bitter, for he had been destined to be the best of the Dragoneers, with his heart of gold and his regal dragon, Royal. Now he only wanted to end them.

Someday he would get the chance. Until then, he would return to his island and the living toys he had there to play with. They would keep him occupied in the meantime.

At least that was what he thought until a few months later, when Rikky, Marcherion, and Aikira came calling.

Neither of the three was ready to forgive Herald's murder, or the torture of innocents.

SEVEN YEARS LATER

Clover watched from Crimzon's back while Jenka helped Jericho pull in the hand-line they were using to fishing. The boy was giggling with delight as the fish slapped its tail on the surface and splashed water into the boat. Zahrellion was on the shore with baby Mystica, their two-year-old daughter.

Crimzon wanted to fly down from their hidden perch and greet them, for he'd grown awfully fond of the Dragoneers while he was helping them, but Clover said it was better to leave them to their happiness. Besides, they'd just gathered up the things they'd come for from the castle, which had been no easy thing to do undetected, especially with that strange, soul-stepping druid guarding over the place like some starving vulture.

Clover had learned from some folks in Three Forks that Rikky was training young men to become rangers at the new Kingsman's Keep, and that he'd personally exiled King Richard to the distant Serpent's Isle, where he and Zahrellion had risked their lives to save him. He'd told King Jenka that if killing Herald Kaljatig in cold blood wasn't reason enough for execution, then it was unarguably reason for exile. The rest of the Dragoneers agreed, and the disturbed young man and his crippled Nightshade were delivered there and all but forgotten.

Marcherion was residing in Kingston most of the time, and he lorded over the islands well enough to keep everyone happy. Lord March, he was called, and he and Rikky loved the hunt as much as their dragons did. Marcherion's anger slid away as the world opened itself to him, mostly because there was no imminent threat for him to battle, but also because the maids and maidens all thought he was a dream and were all trying to seek his favor.

Aikira married an Outland ship's captain named Gareth Chimarrah and had a baby girl with him, but she was still bent on besting Marcherion and Rikky when they hunted the Frontier's open spaces or the inlets along the coast. She and Zahrellion were the best of friends, and Rikky called her Aikira Chimarrah while giggling every chance he got.

Clover was amazed that she was there seeing her Dragoneers at peace with the world and themselves, but she was even more surprised that she was feeling as good as she did.

After nearly dying of age, she and Crimzon found the Leif Repline fountain, in her typical lucky fashion, just in time. After drinking her fill and feeling the aging process start to reverse, she spent two full days hauling buckets of the replenishing liquid out to her dragon. Crimzon could only shiver and complain of the frigid mountain climate as his wounds were healed over anew. He wasn't the worst, though. Listening to the ghost of some dwarven adventurer who'd died in the cavern thousands of years ago was as entertaining as it was maddening. The little bugger had died drunk and seemed to have retained the intoxication in his strange afterlife. He told a great tale, though, when he could get the words out of the slit in his ghostly beard.

They'd only returned here to retrieve some maps Clover had made earlier in her life, and a vial full of a potion she'd gotten on her only trip to the distant continent of Harthgar. These things she had hidden in a place none of the Dragoneers had ever thought to look. She and Crim had a quest waiting on them, but seeing Jenka and his son enjoying the natural bounty of life was as nice an image to behold as she could imagine. Seeing Zahrellion throwing daisies with their little girl on a blanket nearby at the shore was amazing, too. For a long time, the red-haired warrior and her mighty red dragon stayed perched and watched them all.

It was long after the boat had been pulled ashore when she finally urged her dragon to leap into the moonlit sky. They had a long journey across the sea to a place she had never been, but Clover and her dragon were healthy again, as healthy as they'd ever been, and they both had a feeling that all of the Dragoneers, and this land of lost people who were rediscovering the rest of the world, would live happily ever after.

They, on the other hand, were looking for adventure.

After all, the world is but a playground for a girl with a dragon.

The End

BONUS CONTENT:

Crimzon and Clover One—Orphaned Dragon, Lucky Girl

© 2009 By Michael Robb Mathias Jr.

The week-old hatchling nudged its horny head against the cold, lifeless bulk of its mother. Getting no response again, the puny male dragon whined pitifully. Instinctively, he reared his weary head back and squeaked out a high-pitched wail. The sound would have brought a living mother dragon raging home from a hundred leagues or more. A living mother dragon would have stopped at nothing to feed her hatchling's hungry belly. This hatchling wasn't so lucky. His mother was dead. After a long, sorrowful time of nudging and wailing, the song of misery finally ended. Mercifully, the starving little dragon fell into an exhausted slumber.

Being highly intelligent creatures, dragons are taught by their mothers the skills they'll need to thrive in the ever-dangerous world of men. This particular hatchling's mother was now four days dead. She was once the proud and ferocious high predator, and undisputed queen of the small, but very active, range of mountains sheltering her nest. Sadly, her reign had ended.

Years ago, she summoned a mate. His seed readily quickened inside her. She laid her eggs in this remote cavern high up in the rocky passes. Then, as all female dragons do after laying their eggs, she began warning away every living creature that might threaten the welfare of her unhatched young. It wasn't long until every beast in the area, great and small, understood what valleys, caves and streams to avoid, and what the consequences were for not doing so. She then returned to her nest and spent a full year tenderly and methodically incubating the eggs.

When the day of hatching finally came, she proudly coaxed her two little ones out of their shells. She fed them their first meal of red meat from a valley stag she slaughtered. The two baby dragons devoured it greedily. She beamed as they began growling and tumbling with each other all around the gravel-strewn cavern floor. They were working their tender muscles and fluttering their wings awkwardly. Every now and then, one would pause to shriek at the wonder of life and belch out a puff of smoke. More than once a thin tendril of flame accompanied the swirling gray clouds that left the hatchlings' toothy mouths.

On the second day after the hatching, she left them to hunt their next meal. She didn't know how horrible a mistake she was making. She hadn't considered the small group of men traveling through the neighboring valley a viable threat to her nest. Her valley was much higher in elevation, and no man had ever dared venture into it.

In her campaign to warn off possible threats to her eggs, she attacked and terrorized several nearby human towns. She scorched a human dwelling or two, and plundered their animal herds. She devoured a few humans as well. Humans aren't very high up on a typical dragon's preferred sustenance list, but to keep the rest of them frightened and wary of her nest, more than a half dozen men ended up in her belly. In her long life she had been lucky in her dealings with the pesky humans, but her luck in that area, as well as the luck of her two rambunctious hatchlings, was about to run out.

The men came a short while after she left to hunt, and they came with murderous intent. The male hatchling woke to see his nest mate being roped by the angry men. He lashed out at them in a feeble attempt to save his sibling. He clawed one man to the ground and lashed another to the floor with his whip-like tail, but he was too small to do any real damage. Ultimately, he ended up tangled in a throw net the clever humans had brought. The humans paused to argue whether the two young dragons would be taken and sold or killed on the spot. If the mother dragon hadn't returned during the argument, the latter is exactly what would have happened to both of them.

With a single blast of her noxious breath, the mother roared out her anger at the intrusion, scorching several of the men to cinders. Then she unleashed her true fury on them. A purplish-turquoise blast of prismatic dragon magic erupted from her claw and pulverized the bones of two more of the attackers. A blade slid between her scales, but the pain only angered her further. Relentlessly, she went about destroying the men who violated her nest.

The battle that followed was swift and bloody. Though she managed to slay all of the men and save the life of one of her precious young, she took several wounds that couldn't be healed with her magic. Some of the wounds were mortal. She lived just over two days, and in that time she used her remaining energy to try and instill everything she could think of into her surviving hatchling's mind. She wanted to increase his severely slim chances for survival any way she could. She named him Crimzathrion. He was only two days old when the men came, so he understood almost none of his dying mother's melodic ravings, but she wisely cast a spell on her words so they would come to him again and again as he grew. It was all she could do to help him survive in a world full of ignorant men. He would have to find a way to prosper as a hunter while often being hunted himself.

She let Crimzathrion feed on the human bodies she killed, but only because in her wounded condition, she could not hunt for him. She regretted this, because he was so young that he could grow used to the taste of them. She knew a young dragon might mistake the humans for easy prey. Though most of them were generally easy to kill, some were not. Some men were brave, and that made them dangerous. Beyond that, some humans were just plain lucky.

The mother dragon died singing the complex, harmonious songs of magic to the hatchling. She sang the contagious songs of battle, the light and airy songs of flight, and all the songs her own mother sang to her. Then she cursed the Gods for her hatchling's misfortune, as well as for her own. She managed to do more than she ever could have hoped possible to increase her hatchling's chances for survival. She died listening to his persistent whine of hunger, knowing it meant all of the human flesh had been consumed. She couldn't help but cry a tear of sadness for Crimzathrion as she passed into the Everland.

The tear she cried crystallized as it fell. It thudded loudly on the rocky floor. Held inside its sparkling blue beauty was a wealth of magical power, born from love, pain, hope and misery.

Now Crimzathrion lay against her cold, scaly body in a state of partial slumber, exhausted, hungry and afraid. Of all the lessons she'd forced so overwhelmingly upon him, the lesson of death was the one he learned best. He wouldn't get to grow up feeling the immortality of youth. He understood all too well the nature of death, and the magnitude of his loss. He too cried a tear of sorrow that hardened and clacked away across the cavern floor like a shiny pebble.

It wasn't long after his mother's death that her soft voice magically filled his ears. It urged him to go out and hunt for a meal. Feed to grow. Grow to survive. The voice told him. Ravenous with hunger, and with no knowledge of what lay beyond the protective walls of the cavern, he eventually summoned the strength of will to leave his mother's side and do just that.

He screeched out in frustration as he started from the nest to find himself a meal. He was humming the melody to the song of magic as he made his way through the cavern entrance toward the bright and scary light. Crimzathrion didn't know it, but as he stepped into the first sunlight he'd ever known, he was also leaving behind the horrible run of bad luck that the Gods had thrust upon him, for he wasn't alone now.

Far across the valley, a lone traveler, strawberry haired and clad in leather hunting attire, heard the hatchling's long, anguished wails. She was coming as fast as she could to investigate.

Clover Shareon was lucky, to say the least. Some said she was the luckiest human alive. She hadn't the slightest idea what luck really was, but luck was with her this day, as it always seemed to be. She was a third-rate swordsman and a second-rate archer, but a first rate hunter. She knew by heart nearly every peak and valley of this treacherous mountain range. She hunted here for the skins and meat she sold to earn her way. Miraculously, she managed to survive peril after peril over the dozen years she'd been coming here.

Once, the sudden and highly improbable fall of some loose rock and built up ice saved her from being dinner for a pack of hungry snow cats. A deflected fist she once threw at an angry campsite gambler caused her to stumble just out of the way of a surely lethal bolt loosed by the sore loser's friend. She'd been barred from all of the wager houses in the nearby towns because she won too much and far too often. In a battle with road bandits, she'd taken a sword clean through the middle of her belly and survived with only the two scars the blade left on her skin.

Once she fell through a hole in the ice. That was probably the luckiest thing that ever happened to her. She fell only moments before the sleeping wind gusted and sent a massive ridge of loose ice and snow avalanching down into the valley where she was traveling. The hole she fell into turned out to be a tunnel-like shaft that led to an underground cavern. The cave had glowing patches of moss on the walls, illuminating the area well enough to see. There was a spring-fed stream that pooled up in the middle of the bowl-shaped floor. In the pool, schools of eyeless albino fish swam lazily against the mild current. The pool not only provided her with sustenance on her long wait for spring to come and melt away the snow piled above her, but its warm water kept the cavern relatively cozy.

The wailing Clover was hearing now ended suddenly, bringing her back into the moment. She stopped and looked at her surroundings. She was so eager and curious to find the origin of the long, harrowing calls that she lost track of where she was. After a brief moment of panic, she located a familiar peak in the distance and chided herself for her foolishness.

Clover hoped it was a wounded snow cat. Rare and beautiful, their thick, silvery pelts were worth more than she could make in a year guiding traders through the mountains or hunting antelope. Their screeching cries were common enough, but Clover wasn't sure if what she was hearing was a snow cat. The snow cat cries she heard in the past were lower in pitch and more constant. What she heard for the past two days was urgent and higher in tone. It sounded more pain-filled. Snow cat or not, she had to lay her own eyes on whatever it was that sounded so pitiful.

She started toward the sound twice and ended up going in the wrong direction, but both times she was forced back onto the right track by natural obstacles that somehow seemed to help her along the way. Now she was frustrated because the horrible sounds had stopped completely, and she wasn't sure which way to go to continue her search. True to form, luck was with her this day. Out of the corner of her eye, she caught a glinting reflection of scarlet in some trees below her in the valley bottom. She crouched to get a better look, trying not to be seen by the unknown creature. She was disappointed when a mid-size hopper shot out of the undergrowth she was focused on. She laughed, knowing that the melting snow this late in the spring sometimes reflected in crazy colors, but her instincts told her there was something else down there. Some small predator was probably chasing the hopper, or a bigger beast might just be passing through the hopper's territory.

She turned away from the trees below her to look back up the mountain and was stung on the cheek by some tiny insect. As she slapped the pest away, she spun herself back toward the valley and nearly cried out in amazement at what she saw. It was a dragon—a small, red one. It wasn't much bigger than her in body size, though it was longer. It was trying to catch the hopper, clumsily grabbing with its fore claws, while trying in vain to use its small, undeveloped wings to lift itself into flight. Clover felt sorry for the inexperienced hunter, and silently put an arrow to the string of her old bow. She watched until she had a clear shot at the hopper. The young dragon didn't even notice the shaft as it struck his prey and pinned it to the ground. He was too busy pouncing to tear a piece of the long-awaited flesh from it. Clover watched in awe and amazement as the little red wyrm ate its meal.

She wondered suddenly where its mother might be. The huge fire wyrm that sometimes ventured out of the peaks to badger the humans was notorious. She nearly dislocated her neck scanning the skies around her, but the wailing call she'd been hearing the last two days sounded out again from below. It told her on some completely feminine level that no dragon was going to answer the call.

The little dragon's mouth was pink and bloody from the meal, but it was still hungry. It filled the valley with the sound of pain and sorrow. Clover understood that this young dragon was alone—either lost or abandoned—left to fend for itself without the benefit of a mother's nurturing guidance. The sound of the dragon's screeching forced a tear from Clover's eye. She knew in her heart that the little beast had no one in the world and it probably wouldn't survive without help. Clover was careful not to spook the rare, magical young creature as she followed it back up the other side of the valley into a large cavern opening. As she eased into the eerie cave, the stink of death filled her nostrils. It took a while, but she held down her gorge and made her way deeper into the tunnel. Clover's eyes adjusted to the darkness, but they were watering from the fog of rot that hung in the air. When the passage finally opened up into a cavern, she made out a huge mass that nearly filled the place. She had to cover her mouth to keep from screaming in utter terror. Even a weeklong-dead dragon looked horribly scary. Clover found herself trembling as she took in the massive corpse.

Gray, milky eyes the size of wagon wheels, slitted with sword-like pupils, stared out lifelessly. A huge curl of pink tongue split a row of yellowed fangs as big around and as long as Clover's legs. The dead dragon's nostrils were big enough to crawl into and explore. They were like black holes in front of her.

It didn't take long for Clover to spot the cleanly-picked skeletal carcasses of the huge red dragon's killers. They were probably all the little wailing hatchling had eaten before the hopper.

Clover crept back out of the cavern and climbed up on a shelf of rock overlooking the valley below the entrance to the little red's nest. There she set up a well-camouflaged camp. After overcoming her nausea, she ate a thin meal of dried beef and hard bread. Then she started out to hunt some more sustenance for herself and the little dragon.

* * *

Throughout the spring, Clover secretly hunted for her ever hungry, continually growing friend. Each day, she took the time to make the meat harder to find, and if she could, a little larger portion than the day before. By midsummer, the dragon was easily twenty paces long from nose to tail. Though he still wasn't able to lift his growing body with his wings, he could now unfurl them. The dragon could also follow a lengthy blood trail. He started using his hot, fiery breath to char his meat before he ate it, too.

Each day Clover placed something of hers close to the dragon's meals. Her hope was that the dragon would become familiar with her scent. Several times she wanted to approach the creature, but her fear got the better of her. Each day after the dragon would feed, it would sniff around her offering, then return to the now grotesquely pungent nest cave.

One day toward summer's end, Clover came upon a doe elk that had stepped between two fallen logs and broken its foreleg. Clover decided that the dragon was ready to take its first prey for itself. She used a ragged coil of rope to lasso the wounded elk, and with much effort, she pulled the baying and bucking creature over the ridge down into the valley. She felt sad for the elk, knowing that she was leading it to a certain death. It was a wounded and defenseless creature and that weighed upon her. She steeled herself, though. She knew the elk was sure to die in its crippled condition, and she knew the dragon had to learn to hunt and kill on its own. Nature was like that, she reasoned. She told herself she was just helping the inevitable along. She ended up getting the elk well within scent range of the cave opening and then cut the old rope loose. If it could have, the elk would have bolted away in a heartbeat, but its leg was now mangled and useless from fighting Clover's makeshift leash.

Clover said a prayer to the Green Mother for the elk, asking for a quick death for it, as well as for its life to be taken for the good of another. Then she found a good vantage point to watch it all happen and got comfortable.

The young dragon found the elk's scent within minutes, which wasn't easy over the smell of his mother's rotting carcass. He cautiously approached the big elk, moving slowly and sinuously toward the terrified creature. The elk smelled the dragon now and its eyes were rolling and white, full of instinctive panic, yet it stood there like a statue, quivering as the dragon closed in. Then, like a flash, the dragon leapt from the undergrowth and split the elk's neck with a swat of its razor-sharp foreclaw. The wyrm reared back his head and roared out deeply as the smell of fresh blood filled his nostrils and the rush of the kill began to course through his veins.

Crimzathrion took his time cooking and consuming the elk, and more than once he stopped to glance up directly at Clover, but never for long. The fresh meat kept calling him back. Well into evening, the dragon finally finished devouring its first real prey. When he was done, he shook his shiny, red-scaled body, stretched his long, bony spine from neck to tail, then spread his leathery wings wide. After a short, prideful roar, he took a number of long, leaping strides across the clearing and stopped. Several times he did this, each time using his wings a little more effectively. Finally, as the sun was beginning to set, the dragon reared back his head and roared again, this time sending a blast of smoke and flame into the air. Crimzathrion took off running. After only four long strides, he leapt into the air and with a sharp thump of his wings, took his first flight.

Watching this, Clover began to wonder if the dragon needed her anymore. Now that the dragon was able to fly, it would be able to swoop down on its prey like a hawk. The chore of hunting its own food would be easy. She had been yearning to approach the creature and maybe even touch its slick, shiny scales. She heard some dragons could even speak, but figured since this dragon didn't have a mother to teach it, that it probably couldn't. She cursed herself a fool for not approaching it early on while it was still small and timid. Now the dragon was big enough that it could easily kill her if it decided to.

Regretfully, she decided she would make her way back to her camp and pack up so she could move on in the morning. Her friends and family down in town would be missing her, and all of the fools at the Golden Gargoyle Inn would want to drink themselves stupid and listen to her tales. They'd drink toast after toast to her unbelievable luck, and buy her rounds until the barkeep threw them out.

She was lost in thought, staring aimlessly down into the now moonlit valley, when a loud Thrump...Thrump...Thrump from not so far behind and above her split the night. The sound sent her heart hammering through her chest. She spun around, reaching instinctively for her sword. It wasn't there. She remembered she hadn't been carrying it lately. The realization came far too late, for there before her was the dragon, raising his sizable, horned head slowly up to his full, erect height. A long period of dead silence followed. Clover was awed and terrified, but no more than the dragon was. Both were tentative, each taking in the other, until Clover remembered to breathe. As she did, the dragon also sucked in a deep noisy breath of air. Clover held her breath again, half anticipating a blast of flame to shoot forth from the dragon's maw and fry her in her boots, but it never came.

The dragon was trying desperately to find the spell his mother cleverly instilled in his mind that would allow him to speak in the human tongue. He had sensed Clover's presence often. After months of filling his belly on her kills, he knew the human was aiding him. For this he was grateful. He wanted very badly to express his gratitude.

Clover eventually read the curious look in the dragon's eyes and relaxed slightly. She tried to breathe normally but it was useless. Her body was trembling with exhilaration and she was more than just a little bit scared.

"Thank you Green Mother," Clover mouthed to the heavens, but her voice was loud enough for the dragon's keen ears to hear.

The words brought the spell that the dragon was searching for instantly to mind and without thinking he spoke.

"Iss couldss eatss youss," he hissed awkwardly. "Butss yourss kindss tastess bitterss to myss tounge." The dragon then reared his head back, belched out a roiling puff of gray smoke, and made a growling, hacking sound that Clover hoped was some form of laughter.

"Would you bite the hand that feeds you?" Clover asked nervously.

Again the dragon growled and hacked and blew forth smoke. Clover was relieved. This time the corners of the dragon's toothy mouth curled upward and Clover was sure that the expression was one of mirth, not malice.

"I amss owings you humanss." The dragon hissed, his countenance becoming more serious. The hiss in his voice lessened with each word he spoke. "You helpsed me to survives. A gifts I haves for yous, but the gifts must waits."

Clover stood there in awe as the dragon lowered his long neck and body close to the ground, then opened one of his folded wings slightly to give Clover access to his back.

The dragon twisted his long sinuous neck to look back at Clover. "Itss times for uss to flyss, my friends."

Clover's expression was leery. "You said us?"

She really did want to fly on the dragon's back. She had daydreamed of it often while hunting up her scaly friend's meals, but she hadn't forgotten that the dragon had only just flown for the first time, not to mention that it was still fairly small for its kind.

Clover's expression must have revealed her hesitance, for the dragon reared back its head again and roared out his growling, hacking laugh, sending a huge cloud swirling up into the moonlit night. After it recovered from the humor, it turned back to look at Clover.

The dragon chuckled again at the fidgety look on his human friend's face. "It isss ssafe, my friends, I'lls letss no harms comes to youss."

Reluctantly, Clover climbed up onto the dragon. She found that she fit comfortably and snugly between two of the bony spinal plates that protruded down the center of his back. Once she was situated, Clover took a long, deep breath. "My name is Clover. What should I call you?"

"Clo-va," the dragon carefully sounded her name.

"Yes, Clover. What should I call you?"

The dragon thought about this momentarily. "My true name is Crimzathrion. I think it isss to complex for your tonguess to ssspeaks. What woulds you like to calls me?"

Clover patted the dragon's scaly back and smiled as it came to her. "Crimzon is the color of your scales. It's close to Crimz-arthia-rone."

Crimzon chuckled again. "Crimzzzon." The dragon sounded, a hint of satisfaction in his slithery voice. "Yesss… Crimzon iss the color of blood."

Crimzon shifted and raised his body, forcing Clover to grab hold of the bony spinal plate in front of her. The plate's rough, grooved ripples made a perfect handhold for her, and she gripped them just in time. Crimzon was already lunging forward with tremendous force. One ... two ... three ... leaping strides that jarred Clover's teeth together, then there was only weightlessness as smooth as silk. There was a slight lurching sensation for Clover each time Crimzon's huge wings thumped the air, but she didn't even notice. She was too busy holding on for dear life as they nearly clipped the tops of the trees the dragon was struggling to rise above.

The cool, night air rushed over them as they circled slowly upward on Crimzon's strong, steady thrusts. In the dragon's head his mother's soft voice whispered both instruction and encouragement, and the feeling of Clover on his back gave him the confidence and reassurance he needed to avoid falter.

They climbed so high into the sky that Clover thought she just might be able to touch the stars twinkling above them. Her blood was electric with sensation. Her skin was chilled by the rushing air and her stomach was tingling as if full of wiggling snakes. She drew in a deep breath to calm herself, but it was no use. Just as soon as she exhaled Crimzon rolled to the right and then dove sharply, leaving the wiggling snakes from Clover's belly lumped in the back of her throat. Her mind was spinning like a whirlpool.

Far below, the majesty of the moonlit valleys and the hue of colors reflecting from the rocky, snow-capped ridges unfolded before them. Clover marveled at the dozens of rivers and streams that glittered like strands and pools of molten gold. The force of the air pressed hard against her as Crimzon dove. She began to feel dizzy and distant, but before she slipped into unconsciousness, the dragon leveled out and sped across the treetops at such speed that all Clover could see below was a shadowy blur. Soon their momentum died away and Crimzon began to circle and rise again, but now at a more relaxed pace. Clover was glad. She felt rubbery and nauseated. Sick or not, she had to admit that it was the most exhilarating experience she ever experienced.

Before long, Clover spotted her camp. She then felt Crimzon slowing to prepare for landing. As Crimzon glided softly down into the clearing below, Clover saw something out of the corner of her tear-blurred eyes that alarmed her. She was sure it was a trick of the light or caused by the misting in her vision. No way could she have seen a party of men just on the other side of the valley's ridge. At least she hoped not. The sudden loss of inertia and the hard, rough thumping of Crimzon's hind claws slapping and stepping across the valley floor jarred her entire body, pulling her from the troubled thought. She was drenched with an instant feeling of relief that made her forget completely what he might have seen. When they finally came to a halt, she wobbled clumsily from Crimzon's back. On legs as sturdy as water, she crumpled to the ground. Then she howled out in laughter at the wonder she'd just experienced.

Crimzon hacked and growled, and blew smoke from his snout as well. Later, after they finally settled down from the thrill of the flight, Crimzon ventured down into the putrid lair. The smell of his mother's rotting body was far too strong for Clover to handle, so she was forced to wait outside and wonder curiously what the gift was that the young dragon planned to give her. She didn't feel that the dragon owed her anything; the flight alone had been payment enough.

The dragon returned shortly, carrying something gingerly in his foreclaw. It appeared to be a large, fist-sized jewel. Crimzon explained that it was a dragon's tear—his mother's tear—and he presented it to Clover with much emotion.

For a moment, when it was first in her hands, Clover didn't understand. But then it hit her like a bolt of lightning. The powerful magic held inside the tear exploded inside of her, filling her with rush after surging rush of energy and heat. It took her breath and filled her head with colorful collages of incomprehensible visions, each having a distinct meaning, one blurring into another. Due to the intensity of the tear's magic, Clover nearly let it fall from her hands, but somehow she managed to hold on. When the electric sizzling in her blood finally settled, she was something and someone else altogether. Not physically—no, she was still Clover on the outside—but inside her head, spell after spell swirled and danced, as did eons of knowledge and understanding, not only of the race of Dracus, but of all the races of the world. She was just about to say the ancient words of acceptance, words that she had never read or heard anywhere before in her life, when a thick flight of arrows came raining down on them from above.

The shouts and excited calls of human warriors filled the air, and more arrows came raining down.

Whether it was her luck or the protective magic of the tear, Clover was miraculously missed. It might have been that she wasn't the target that the men were aiming for.

Crimzon howled in pain. He was hit nearly a dozen times, but only one or two of the steel-tipped wooden shafts managed to penetrate his thick, scaly hide. He wasted no time taking back to the air where he could quickly fly beyond the archers' range. Still he was pelted and pierced several more times before he got very far.

Clover charged relentlessly toward the cover of the cavern. The air inside the shaft hit her like a blanket of rot. She felt she should do something, but wasn't sure what or how. It was a chore just to draw a breath. By the time an idea came to her, she was pinned in the cavern by a pair of archers, who were loosing arrow after arrow into the entrance. At a glance she counted at least half a dozen chainmail-clad swordsmen coming swiftly behind them.

"We don't want you, fool", an angry voice called out. "All we want is the old dragon's hoard."

Hoard, Clover thought. There was no hoard here. This was Crimzon's mother's nest, not her lair. Her hoard could be anywhere. She shook her head in confusion. Until she had held the tear she had known nothing of such things. "There's no hoard here, man!" She yelled back at them. "This was a nest!" She was answered with a pair of arrows that came so close to her head that she heard them whoosh by her ears.

"Come on, wench," growled a raspy voice as hard as granite. "Come out of there so we can handle our business."

"Yeah," another voice added, "Or you'll become our business! Ain't that right, Captain?"

* * *

Outside, Crimzon was circling above the attackers, taking in the scene below him. Twenty men he counted, plus some who had already gone inside his mother's resting place. They were trying to do harm to his human friend, and he didn't know what he should do. He knew he was wounded, but he didn't care about that. He wanted to help Clover, but was too afraid. He rose even higher, then cleared the ridge and swooped down into the valley adjacent to the one where the men were. There he found a small cavern opening. He landed near its mouth and squeezed and wiggled his way inside, snapping off several of the arrows sticking out of him as he went.

* * *

Clover was feeling as unlucky as could be. In the dark cavern where Crimzon's mother lay rotting, she hid on an elevated shelf that she found. From there she was trying to assess the situation. Her eyes adjusted to the blackness quickly, and she could make out at least ten heavily armored swordsmen. Every one of them was coughing and gagging. A couple of archers and what Clover figured to be a mage were moving into the cavern as well. Any sound or motion she made would give her position away. The mage chanted something that Clover inexplicably knew to be a light spell, then suddenly a glowing sphere of pastel color appeared, hovering above the man's upturned palm. The inside of the cavern was thrust into its eerie, blue glow.

Clover shrank back into the shadows as two of the swordsmen began to vomit from the sight of the huge, decomposing dragon. The mage began to chant another spell that somehow cleared the putrid stench form the place and replaced it with clean, fresh air.

Clover felt the dragon's tear pulsing in her hand, but she wasn't sure how to unleash its power. The spells were in her head, but not the knowledge of how to cast them, or the ill effects of their castings. She wondered what happened to Crimzon. Did the young dragon get scared and run away, or was he wounded and dying? The thought that he was outside, fighting for his life irked her. Clover decided if he had flown away scared, she couldn't blame him. After all, Crimzon wasn't even a yearling, and after watching humans such as these kill his mother, it was understandable for him to be afraid. Still, Clover hoped that Crimzon was alright, and she wished her scaly friend was there to help her fight off these greedy treasure seekers.

"Come on now, wench," the hard-voiced leader of the group yelled out into the open air of the place. His voice reverberated heavily off the stone. "We won't harm you if you just come out."

Captain Harner was the self-proclaimed leader of this fairly well-organized band of glory seekers. He was an efficient predator in his own right. Whether it was other men, mountain creatures, or seemingly evil dragons that he faced, he showed no fear and maintained order among his men. Most importantly, he always got them paid for their work. He had no qualms poaching exotic game or selling little girls to the bathhouses. He picked his conquests clean, squeezing every last copper from them. He just wanted Clover to show herself so one of his archers could pierce her heart. He had high hopes of finding coins and jewels in the dragon's horde, but he could already tell this wasn't a lair.

He accepted the fact that this wasn't where the dragon kept its treasure, but he still had to pay his men. Picking a single wench clean didn't seem like much, but it beat a total loss. He had seen some dragon piles in a valley a few ridges back. He was hoping it meant the lair was close by. The foolish woman hiding in here might know where it is. If not, her supplies might provide enough loot to fund a few more days up here in the mountains to search it out.

"Come on out, woman!" The Captain ordered again. "Stop wasting my time!"

It was the mage who found Clover first. He cast a spell that sensed the presence of magic other than his own. When he sensed the dragon's tear in Clover's hand, he began to panic, for it radiated more power than he could imagine. This caused him to hold his tongue and stare openly at Clover instead of calling out an alarm.

Clover knew she'd been seen. It was just a matter of time now before the mage blasted her with lightning, put her to sleep, or cast some other type of spell to incapacitate her. Either way, she was spotted, so she decided to gamble.

"Don't kill me, and I'll show you to the lair," Clover yelled as she stood up and showed herself. "I know where it is," she added convincingly, "I swear it!"

"Don't shoot!" Captain Harner yelled instantly. "Hold your arrows!"

The Captain ordered his archers to keep their shafts trained on Clover while his swordsmen made a half circle around the elevated shelf his victim was on. "You lie, you die, fool!" The Captain said through gritted teeth as he approached. He didn't notice the look of apprehension on his mage's face. If he had sensed the amount of awe and fear the mage was feeling, he might have kept a little distance. As it was, he approached the chin-high scallop in the cavern wall swiftly and authoritatively.

"Tell me," said the Captain, whose voice was now hard but reasonable, almost reassuring. "Where is this lair?"

"I'll not say," Clover returned sharply, "but I'll show you for an equal share."

"An equal share she wants!" The Captain mocked, bringing a few grunts of laughter from his men. Suddenly he threw a dagger so quickly that Clover only felt it as its keen edge nicked open her ear lobe. "You'll show me, or you'll die a slow, miserable death, wench! These men won't be kind to your body, I assure you," the Captain growled. "Get the chains!" He ordered, then pointed at Clover. "Come down from there now, or my archers will take out your legs."

Clover tried to relax. She hoped Crimzon had gotten far away from here. She was sure the young dragon would be hunted down and killed for his hide as soon as this crazy mercenary learned she had no idea where the lair was. Clover tucked the dragon's tear discreetly into her belt pouch while turning to climb down from the shelf. Luckily no one noticed this. The warriors wasted no time crowding her in and grabbing her wrists as she stepped down. She was overcome by a wave of defeat. A sharp punch in her gut sent her air, and most of what little hope of survival she had been holding back, whooshing out of her. She fell, crumpled between the two huge men who effortlessly held her from completely collapsing. Out of a breathless mouth she silently called for Crimzon to come save her. It seemed to her that the incredible run of good fortune she was on had finally petered out.

* * *

Crimzon was only moments away from his friend when her weak voice spoke magically into his mind. Little did Clover know, but all spring Crimzon had been going out another tunnel that led from the cavern out into the adjacent valley. He had been hunting and killing his own prey and exercising his wings for flight. He even scared a herd of fleet deer over the ridge when game ran scarce for Clover. Clover often wondered how the dragon had grown so large so quickly on such a meager diet. If she had known about the other tunnel, she would have had her answer. Crimzon made it into a game. He watched Clover hunt and place her kills for him many times. He often wondered why a human would do such a thing for his kind. Crimzon eventually concluded that not all humans could be like the ones who killed his mother. After months of Clover's persistent, though unnecessary aid, Crimzon came to like his human benefactor.

He wanted nothing more now than to help her. After he squirmed his long, scaly body through the last tight corner of the other cavern way, he drew in a long, deep breath. It wasn't only air he was pulling into his vast lungs, but courage as well. He would be there for Clover; he only hoped he could get there in time.

* * *

"Lift her up," Captain Harner barked. "Raise up her head!"

A heavy fist grabbed a handful of her strawberry hair and pointed Clover's face directly at the rugged Captain. Their eyes locked, and Clover's hope for bluffing dissipated like a puff of pipe smoke in a gale. The Captain's eyes were nearly empty. Only a glint of hatred and a sparkle of greed shone in those icy orbs. Clover was about to die, and she knew it. The feeling was confirmed when the Captain's sword point deftly found her throat.

"I'll ask you only once," the Captain hissed with narrow, angry brows. "Tell me the location of the dragon's lair, or swallow my steel!"

Clover gulped. She felt a trickle of blood drip down her neck. It was a warm sensation that chilled her with terror. Her eyes darted from angry face to leering, angry face. In those gazes she found nothing but an eagerness to see her blood. She was about to blurt out a lie when two things stopped her. One was the Captain's blade point pushing firmly into her neck; the other was a shift in the shadows beyond the Captain.

"She doesn't know, Captain," a voice spat excitedly. "Kill her! Or better yet, let me have her!"

"Aye, Captain, those boots we found in her camp would look good on my wife," said another.

Like a snake sliding through tall grass a thin, raspy voice cut through the grunts of approval for Clover's execution. "There's a way to find out for sure," said the mage.

"I see you still have your wits about you, magic man," the Captain said coolly. "Tell us if she knows or if she'll die here by my blade."

The mage began chanting rhythmically, waving his arms around. This went on for a few minutes. Then he paused as still as stone, made a choking grunt, and fell over. Everyone present, even the Captain and Clover, stared at the mage's lifeless body as if they expected him to jump back up any minute. The mage's sphere of glowing blue light began to slowly fizzle out, causing a sense of panic to sweep over the hardened men. Clover felt the grips on her wrists tighten considerably.

"What is it, Captain?" A shaky voice called out.

"Yeah, what killed the spell caster?" Asked another.

"Shhh!" The captain hissed. "Find a torch before we run completely out of light."

The Captain turned and pointed toward something with his sword, allowing Clover to breathe again. Clover squeezed her eyes shut and fearfully began a silent prayer to the Green Mother. It was a typical stroke of luck that her eyes closed when they did, for a brilliant, white-hot shower of blazing dragon's breath came down over the unsuspecting Captain, cooking his vitals to char in less than a heartbeat. The intense heat and brightness of it told Clover to keep her eyes closed. She could smell her own hair burning and wasn't sure if she would be burned as well, but a reassuring voice in her head told her not to worry, to stay still and be ready to escape the cavern.

Crimzon came back to help her, after all. When the bright heat finally disappeared, Clover felt one hand let go of her. She spun, twisted, and brought her knee up into her other captor's groin. Then she swung an overhand right into the warrior's helmet.

She felt her hand bones shatter from the impact, but she also felt the man's gripping hand fall away.

The eyes of most of the mercenaries were flash blinded by the dragon's breath. To them the cavern was nothing but bright, splotchy blackness. Since Clover kept her eyes closed, her sight was not as bad. With a little concentration, she was able to make out her surroundings in the dark.

As Crimzon's bone-chilling battle roar echoed through the cavern, Clover looked around and saw the way she had to go to get out. She bolted up the shaft she had come down. An instant later, shouts, screams, and more blinding blasts of fire filled the chamber behind her.

All of the young dragon's pent-up rage and his hatred for the men who killed his family came out as he unleashed his fury upon the men. With the mage dead, he didn't have to fear a magical attack, so he let his battle lust take over his senses. With his breath he blasted man after man, and with the crushing force of his long tail, whipped another against the wall. With a swipe of his claw he raked a trio of deep furrows across a man, then snapped his toothy maw shut on another. A sword bit into his scales and opened his flesh, but he gouged the swordsman with one of the spikes on his head and mashed his bones against the cavern wall.

Clover chanced to look back to see how Crimzon was faring. By the sounds of it all, the men didn't have a chance. By the look of it, Crimzon already wounded or killed most of them. A few men were fleeing up the tunnel toward Clover. She took this as a sign to move faster, and move she did. It was only about three hundred more paces through open tunnel to get out of the cavern into the valley, but to Clover's frustration, the way was blocked by two more men; men who hadn't yet seen the dragon, and were watching Clover approach through confused and excited eyes.

The men before her heard the dragon as well as the clash of steel on scale and stone. Instinctively they wanted to run, but to disobey the captain was death, so they held their ground. When they saw Clover wasn't one of them, they quickly moved to block her way.

Clover reached for her sword but found only the lump of the dragon's tear in her belt pouch. She didn't know why, but she fumbled for it as she charged on. When her fingers finally wrapped around it, the rush of power that filled her nearly dropped her in her tracks. Of its own accord, her broken hand shot forth and a jagged string-thin bolt of sizzling yellow shot from her fingertip into the chest of one of the men blocking her way. The man convulsed and fell trembling to the side, and before this even registered in Clover's mind, the other man was in even worse condition. She didn't even have to slow her pace. She hurdled their bodies in stride and kept running toward the moonlight. When she burst out into the valley bottom, she found another group of men, mostly archers, waiting there. They were as startled as she was. She would have been riddled with arrows had her luck not held true. One of the archers had snuck along a few skins of brandy and the men were half drunk and un-alert when Clover charged through their camp.

When their comrades came out of the cavern, they went scrambling clumsily for their bows. Several of the men emerging from the cave were torn and bleeding. One was smoldering and missing an arm. Red embers flared on the end of his stumped elbow as he stumbled headlong from the cavern and sprawled onto the ground.

"The Captain's dead!" A terrified voice called out.

"The dragon's coming behind us!" Another yelled. "Archers, be ready!"

Had it been the Captain's voice, they would all have continued scrambling for their bows. Instead they stood there, slack-jawed and shocked as Crimzon came loping out of the cavern. A screeching blast of fire finished off the armless man as well as the man trying to help him. From another direction, a crackling strand of yellow erupted from Clover's finger tip and electrified another man where he stood.

A few of the mercenaries managed to get to their weapons and fire arrows back at Crimzon and Clover. But after Crimzon snatched up a man with his toothy maw and violently shook him in half, the others turned and fled, leaving everything behind save for themselves.

Only a single man of the Captain's party remained. He was still down in the cavern. He had hidden in the rocks when the dragon showed up. He found the tiny, crystal-blue dragon's tear Crimzon cried so many months ago. Mistaking it for a jewel, he pocketed it. The rush of power he felt was nowhere near as powerful or intense as Clover's had been, but the man felt it just the same and knew his destiny lay elsewhere. He stole the coin purses off several of his fallen comrades, then quietly slinked away into the tunnel from where Crimzon emerged to surprise them.

In the valley, after all the surviving men fled, Crimzon lifted his head proudly and let out a trumpeting roar of dominance that curdled even Clover's blood. When he was done, the dragon bowed before Clover and lowered his wing to allow her to mount his back.

"Comes Clovers, let's hunts them down!" Crimzon hissed vengefully.

"Do you think it's necessary?" Clover asked, feeling the throb of pain in her hand starting to lessen.

"They will tellss taless and brings back otherss if we do not!" Crimzon rationalized.

"Yes," Clover reluctantly agreed, "but this place can't be your … our home forever. There's a whole world beyond these mountains."

"Yessss, Clover," Crimzon growled. "but climb upon me ands we wills chase them as they go. Theys deserves no easy escapess."

Clover climbed on and had just gotten situated when Crimzon jumped into the air in a single leaping stride. On powerful surging wing strokes the young red dragon, and a very lucky woman, chased away the bad men. After that was done, they decided to explore beyond the mountains.

Crimzon and Clover would have many more adventures. Some you might hear about in a tavern or in a bard's tale like this one. After all, the world is but a playground for a girl with a dragon.

The End (for now)

Don't miss the huge International Bestselling epic series:

The Wardstone Trilogy

Book One - The Sword and the Dragon
Book Two - Kings, Queens, Heroes, & Fools
Book Three - The Wizard & the Warlord

Also by M.R. Mathias

The Saga of the Dragoneers:

The First Dragoneer—Free Novella
The Royal Dragoneers
Cold Hearted Son of a Witch
The Confliction
Confliction Compendium
The Emerald Rider

The Crimzon and Clover Short Story Series

Crimzon & Clover I - Orphaned Dragon, Lucky Girl
Crimzon & Clover II - The Tricky Wizard
Crimzon & Clover III - The Grog

Crimzon & Clover IV - The Wrath of Crimzon

Crimzon and Clover V—Killer of Giants

Oathbreaker - A Faery Tale Short

King of Fools

The Adventurion

ROAR—A Wardstone Short

The Blood of Coldfrost—A Wardstone Short

To learn more about these titles and the author and to find several free reads please visit: www.mrmathias.com